OLE

MOSCOW

BERLIN

BAGHDAD

PARIS

ROME

AROUND ROCKALL
OF 250 MILES.
AT INTERVALS OF
LES

THE MASTER

THE MASTER

An Adventure Story

by

T. H. WHITE

London

JONATHAN CAPE　30 BEDFORD SQUARE

FIRST PUBLISHED FEBRUARY 1957
SECOND IMPRESSION 1957

PRINTED IN GREAT BRITAIN IN THE CITY OF OXFORD
AT THE ALDEN PRESS
BOUND BY A. W. BAIN & CO. LTD., LONDON

To the happy memory of

GONZALO: I' the commonwealth I would by
contraries execute all things . . .
No sovereignty,—

SEBASTIAN: Yet he would be King on't.

ANTONIO: The latter end of his commonwealth forgets the beginning.

— *The Tempest*

Contents

Contents

THE MASTER

The Yellow Hands

It was a blistering day in July, and the swell of the sea was like melted lemonade bottles.

The twins lay face down on the hot rock, dressed in nothing but overalls. Nicky was squinting at some stars or pin-points of light, which the sun threw on the glittering stone three inches from his nose. By letting his eyes go out of focus, these could be made to swim slowly to the left. Judy was fiddling with a broken egg-shell, admiring its thin, curved, fragile smoothness.

In the blue, unwinking sky above them — unwinking but it made you blink — dozens of sea birds were whirling and circling like snow flakes. As they came between you and the sun, they went brown, then black, and you could see through their wing feathers.

The children's father was sitting with Mr. Pierrepoint on the slanting shelf about twenty feet away.

They had their backs turned and were eating sandwiches.

Mr. Pierrepoint had a coloured shirt with pictures of Balinese dancing girls painted on it in mauve and electric green. The Duke was dressed in his one-piece rompers, like Sir Winston Churchill's, but his were made of water-proofed cheese-cloth. He had a theory about being porous. He had an oil-skin hat too, like the man in the advertisement for "Scotts Emulsion". Both of them were in good humour.

"My dear sir," the Duke was saying, "do you realize that ours may be the first of human feet to scale this craglet of the wine-dark sea, what?"

"Come again?"

"We are the first people to land here."

"Duke," said Mr. Pierrepoint, "it says in the book that St. Brendan landed here, on his way to discover the States. He was sailing on a mill-stone at the time, and he called the rock by the name of Brandion."

"I know, my dear fellar, I know. But . . . "

"It says . . . "

The twins stopped listening.

Judy put down the egg-shell and said, "All the same, Nicky, it does feel queer."

"What feels queer?"

"Being the First Human Feet."

"I bet we're not, anyway. What about in the last war? All the aircraft went over it — I know that, at any rate. Daddy's information always seems to stop at about 1896."

"Nicky!"

"Well, it does. And how could St. Brendan have floated on a mill-stone?"

"Its supposed to be poetical, I suppose. Or religious."

He made one of his sea-faring noises.

16

The cliff on which they were basking was the island of Rockall, which comes in the weather forecasts. It is a granite peak, about seventy feet high, hardly bigger than a large house, and it juts out of the enormous, heaving, lonely Atlantic, some two hundred and fifty miles north-west from the nearest tip of Ireland.

Once it was part of Atlantis — perhaps — before that continent sank beneath the waves.

Round it, the abyss falls further than the thousand fathom line. Its fang of stone in the wilderness of water is the single speck which rises above the surface between Britain and America. It is the very home of sun and spray and solitude.

It is true that few people have landed there. For one thing, its loneliness used to make it difficult to find by navigation. For another, it is difficult to land on, being precipitous and often covered by the waves.

Apart from the legendary St. Brendan, Rockall has been mentioned a few times in history. Frobisher saw it once, in the spacious days. At that time it was actually wooded, so it must have been higher and larger then. In 1810, a Captain Hall of H.M.S. *Endymion* saw the white droppings of the sea-birds on its summit and mistook these for a snowy topsail — so he gave it chase. The landing party which he sent to investigate was cut off by a sudden fog. (Fogs were another of the things which made it difficult to find Rockall. It was not easy in those days to sail 250 miles on a compass bearing and hit a dot which was only seventy feet high.)

Then there was a brigantine called the *Helen*, which was wrecked on an outlying reef in 1824. It is called Helen's Reef even now. But it is strange that a ship should have collided with something no bigger than a ship, in the desert of the Atlantic Ocean. It is as if two fleas walking across a ballroom floor should meet end on.

In 1862, the boatswain of H.M.S. *Porcupine* was sent with a boat's crew to try to scale the place. It was a tossing swell when they came alongside, so no landing was possible. But he managed to grasp a fragment of the island as they rose and fell. He knocked it off with his sounding lead. They brought the bit back to England. It is in the British Museum.

In 1896 — the date which Nicky mentioned — the Royal Irish Academy organized an expedition specially to land there. It made two attempts, at a fortnight's interval, but both attempts were beaten off by the heave of the sea, which was as high as the Himalayas.

Since then, a French research ship has visited and broken off a piece of Rockallite, without being able to land — in 1921 — and a Mr. M. T. Bizony swam round the crag on a float lowered from the Fleetwood trawler *Bulby* in 1948. He also managed to chip off some.

As is well known, Great Britain annexed Rockall on September 18th, 1955, with a salute of 21 guns. This may have been a result of what I am going to tell you.

The reason why Mr. Pierrepoint and the Duke had come was so that they could say they had seen such a seldom visited spot, and had managed to land on it.

People do these things without more particular causes.

One of the men who tried to climb Everest was asked why he did, and replied, "Because it is there."

Mr. Pierrepoint's skipper had found the rock by good navigation and they had scaled it by good luck — using a harpoon gun to throw a rope ashore.

They had been lucky with the weather.

In the offing, the big yacht with its yellow funnel and clipper-like lines — it had a sort of bowsprit — moved slowly round in the sunlight, the skipper worrying about reefs. They could see the Duchess on the sundeck under a red parasol, reading about palmistry, and her Irish setter called Sherry curled up beside her — a brown speck not interested in islands. At the foot of the crag on the west side, the ship's boat lifted and sank like a lift on the breathing bosom of the ocean. The disturbed birds circled above them in the fizzling aether. People have claimed to see on or near Rockall: Razor-bills, Puffins, Gannets, Kittiwakes, Guillemots, Fulmars, two kinds of Skuas, Manx Shearwaters and even the Greater Shearwaters which nest on Inaccessible Island in the South Atlantic. As a matter of fact, it was once believed that the Greater Shearwater nested on Rockall, but of course this is nonsense. No birds nest there.

With an oceanic "fetch" of thousands of miles — all the way from America — the local waves during great gales are at least sixty feet from crest to trough. Breaking surf — the water thrown up on meeting obstructions — goes to hundreds of feet. (The lighthouse at Dunnet Head on the Pentland Firth which is more or less in the Rockall area, stands on a cliff three hundred feet high — yet its windows have often been broken by wave-thrown stones.) These grand storms come four or five times a year. So how could any sensible bird nest on a crag only seventy feet above the surface?

But they do visit the place and they do rest on it.[1]

The Duke had brought a geological hammer with him, determined to out-do the boatswain of the *Porcupine*, and now he set to work.

The noise of his chopping mingled with the strange cries of the gulls.

There was one other living thing on Rockall, and this was Judy's mongrel bitch, whose name was Jokey. They had called her Jokey when she was a puppy, because she really did seem a joke, and a bad one at that. She was such a muddle that all her legs seemed to be of different sizes. She had a long tail, and hair in her eyes, and her coat mostly grew the wrong way, like a hyena's. She looked like a small, untidy, busy charwoman, who had been born in a dustbin. She was about the size of a Skye terrier. Judy loved her more than anything on earth. At the moment, she was yapping.

"Where's Jokey?"

They had to raise their voices because of the gulls.

"She went down there."

"Jokey!"

They whistled and shouted without result, getting

[1] After this novel was in the hands of the printers, an interesting book on Rockall was published by Mr. James Fisher (Geoffrey Bles, 18s.), which gives more facts about the island than were known to the author at the time of writing.

only yaps and silences in answer — the silences being for investigation and the yaps for help.

"She must have found something."

"It's probably only a dead bird."

"Jokey!"

"Oh, she is a nuisance," said Judy. "She has probably got herself cliffed or something, and can't get back."

Indeed, the south-east side of Rockall was almost a precipice and they were lying on the edge of it. Or rather, it was two cliffs with a sort of step between them — the top cliff being about twenty feet and the lower one about fifty. There were fairly good foot- and hand-holds — good enough for children anyway, who are lighter in proportion to their energy than adults are.

"Jokey!"

"I suppose I shall have to go and see."

"She's all right."

"But she might fall off."

"Don't *fuss*."

You could almost see what the twins were thinking, as they lay face downwards. Judy was thinking, "Nicky is a man and ought to go, because men do things for women, except cooking." Nicky was thinking, "It is her dog anyway."

"You would be sorry if she was killed."

"No, I wouldn't."

"Nicky!"

"Why should she be killed?"

"Because it's dangerous."

"Well, go and find her then."

"You ought to go."

"Why ought I?"

"Because."

But it was unanswerable really, for everybody knew that Jokey was Judy's.

There was a resentful silence, except for the saw-mill cries of the Gannets and the clop of the hammer. In the distance, one of the Gannets on coastal patrol spotted a submarine fish, poised for a moment on stalling wing, and fell like a plummet, a thunderbolt, a dive-bomber. It went straight into the sea, plonk, and the little, white fountain of water rose behind it almost lazily into the sparkling air. You could count four slowly, and then there was the dark-looking head on the surface, shaking itself, swallowing the fish. Others of the squadron came to the signal, for it was evidently a shoal, and they peeled off, one after the other, plonk, plonk, plonk. Beautiful dives!

Judy got up complainingly — "a woman's work is never done" — and began to pick her way among the sharp ledges of the rock. Soon she had worked her way round a shoulder of the cliff and vanished.

"Nicky!"

The thin call mixed with the bird noises.

"What?"

"Come here."

"Why?"

"Please come."

"Oh, all right."

He used his grudging voice automatically, but jumped up willingly enough, because as a matter of fact he had wanted to go all the time. Only he had not known that he wanted to.

"What is it?"

"Come and see."

Just below the ledge or step in the cliff face, and clinging rather precariously to a kind of natural shelf or pathway, Judy and Jokey were absorbed in something in front of their noses. Both noses were pointing at it, like the noses of setters, and Jokey's head was on one side, the ears cocked forward.

Nicky made his way down the steepness of granite, putting the shoulder of Rockall between himself and his father. The noise of the hammer died away. Even the cries of birds seemed to fall silent. Now both children were out of sight and out of hearing, even of the yacht.

"What is it?"

"Oh, shut up, Jokey. Don't yap."

The ledge was broad enough to stand on, so she picked the dog up, struggling, and held its mouth shut with her fingers. Jokey was furious.

"It's something in there."

"Where?"

"*Jokey!*"

Kneeling down in the professional way which men have when they are called to mend the plumbing or find out what has gone wrong with the kitchen stove, Nicky examined the rock face where the dog had been sniffing. It was as if the three of them were standing on the keyboard of an upright stone piano. The cliff rose in front of them, where you put the music, and fell behind them to the pedals in the sea.

As a matter of fact, it was more like an enormous pianola. Behind the music rack in these, there is a panel which can be opened, to see the dotted music going round its drums. And straight in front of Nicky, cut in the living rock with the exactness of a cabinet maker, there were the ruled slits or cracks of what looked like a pair of garage doors.

The doors or whatever they were, were not smoothed or planed outside. They were rough and chunky like the rest of the cliff. They had no handles or bolts or visible means of opening them. From a few paces away you could not see the cracks. It was as if a giant with a sharp knife had cut a mathematical square in the side of the island, like cutting a slice of cake without taking the piece out.

"Gee!"

"Jokey says there is something inside."

"It can't be in the crack, Judy. Look, it goes straight up and straight along and down again. And look, it splits in the middle. It must be sort of doors."

"But what's it for?"

"It must be made by men. If it was Nature, it wouldn't be straight lines."

He ran his fingers along the crack, fascinated by the discovery. Judy, who was about twice as quick on the uptake as Nicky was, began to feel scared.

"Let's go and tell Daddy."

"No, wait a minute. I want to see. Look, if they opened outwards, there would be grooves in the ledge here for them to swing on. They must go inwards. Wait, I want to push."

She stood doubtfully, clutching the wriggling mongrel to her chest, disapproving of the whole affair.

"Let's get Daddy first."

But Nicky was busy shoving at the cliff.

"They must be locked."

"Perhaps they are just natural," she said hopefully, "the result of an earthquake or something? Or a volcano?"

"Ass."

"But Nicky . . . "

At this point one of the doors opened of its own accord, smoothly and ponderously, like the door of a heavy safe.

A pair of yellow hands, with long fingernails like a mandarin's, came from the dark interior — and courteously pushed both children off the cliff.

CHAPTER TWO

Inside

WHEN the Duke and Mr. Pierrepoint had searched and scrambled and hollered for half an hour, they were rowed back to the yacht for help. The yacht steamed round the islet, with her binoculars searching the stony faces and the sea below. A landing party was sent to examine every inch once more. But the eyes of adults and even the magnification of binoculars at a distance were not so sharp as the eyes of children, and human noses were not so delicate as Jokey's. Nobody noticed the cracks in the rock. In the end they came back with Judy's red straw hat, found floating in the water.

It would be kinder not to think of the scene on board — the Duchess rigid and motionless like a statue, but her fingers moving of their own accord, tearing up a handkerchief — the poor Duke with his grey head in his hands, huddled in the stateroom, staring at the floor. Mr. Pierrepoint, who was the Duchess's brother, was as wretched as anybody.

He said, "Fanny, it was an accident. You were not to blame."

The yacht stayed for two days scanning the sea. Then she steamed away. There was nothing else to do.

When Judy went backwards off the ledge, still clutching Jokey to her bosom, they both squealed on exactly the same note.

Nicky shouted, "Look out!"

Now this was odd. He shouted it *to himself*.

He saw the cliff face streaming past him like the road going under a fast car or — to go back to the pianola — like the slotted music whirling backwards on the drum, when you press the knob to re-wind. He also saw — for he was seeing in all directions at the same time — the green and twinkling sea shooting up towards him, with all the little wavelets crinkled on the bigger wave, and oval sunspots scattered on the highlights, and the smallness of distance growing and enlarging and expanding and engulfing as it rose to meet him. And then, with a smashing whoosh and an agonizing slash across his eyelids and up his nose, he was down, down, down, in the viridian, choking, smothering, salty, stunning water. He hung in it, struggling like a dog, half insensible, holding his breath, not sure which was up or down. He was too busy to think of death. In the deep silence he made a guess for upwards and wrestled towards it, paddling desperately, panting without breath, striving to do, to survive.

His lungs were bursting. The light was going reddish. He was going to have to take a breath of brine.

Then, with a gasp, still threshing his arms, shaking his head like a wet otter, he was out in the sunlight.

His whole face was smarting as if someone had brutally slapped it, and his chest, bare except for the overalls, and the underside of his arms, were red and tingling. He could hardly see.

Next moment, Judy popped up beside him.

The moment after that, Jokey appeared.

Judy, looking cross, blew out a mouthful of sea and instinctively put up a hand to smooth her streaming hair. Jokey, looking oddly thin with a small, wet, skull-face like a drowned rat's, decided that the safest and dryest place would be on top of Judy. She put her forepaws on the girl's head, began to climb up, and both sank spluttering beneath the wave, fast by their native shore.

When they came up again, entangled, Judy was exasperated.

"How could you!"

She put down the whole affair to Jokey, as she needed somebody to blame. She slapped the dog clumsily and sank for the second time.

They got back to the surface in a better mood. Poor Jokey's panic-stricken paddling had touched Judy's heart. This time she took the frightened paws on her shoulders of her own accord, holding the little body close with one arm, and trod water. Jokey's wet, wild face looked left and right and left again, hating what seemed to be a mad bath night.

Nicky was going to say, "Who did that?", when more things began to happen.

There were plops in the sea beside them, which did not seem connected with three or four loud bangs above their heads. The noise could not be heard on the opposite side of the cliff.

Nicky looked up, peering through his swollen eyes, and there, fifty feet above his head, the door of rock was open. The Chinaman — for it was a Chinaman and in a saffron robe too, with blue dragons on it — was standing there and calmly shooting at them with an automatic pistol.

Shooting at them!

Nicky was indignant. First to push you off a cliff and then to shoot at you! It was dangerous. The funny thing was that he was not frightened. He thought, *This is disgraceful! People can't do this sort of thing to me!*

And then, while the dragon man was still potting and Jokey was whimpering and Judy was wondering what was making the plops, a second door in the sheer precipice opened in front of them at sea level — this time a smaller door, more like a window — and there appeared in it a gigantic, coal-black negro.

Judy, who was facing in the opposite direction, remarked in a detached way: "Nicky, I think somebody is throwing things at us."

The negro dived — a superb, professional dive with the curve of a salmon's leap. In two strokes, he was behind her back and had seized her by the hair. Judy opened her mouth — so did Jokey — and both at once, with their mouths open, sank for the third time. As they went down, they rolled their eyes.

Two more strokes took the man back to the opening with his cargo in tow, where several pairs of willing hands hoisted the dripping bodies over the sill. The blackamoor swung round in the water, almost colliding with Nicky, who had been paddling doggedly behind. In less time than it takes to tell, the boy also had been heaved inside, the blackamoor had followed him in a shower of drops, and the heavy door or casement had swung silently behind them into place.

They stood, streaming with water, in a tiled corridor lit by electric light.

One of the straps of Nicky's overalls was burst. Judy's trousers had split right up the outside seams. Jokey shook herself vigorously over the nearest dry person, as wet dogs always do, and said, "So much for that."

Nobody spoke.

There were six men in dungarees with grease-stains on them, who stood looking at the children in silence. The negro, wreathed in smiles, nodded and gurgled, making patting movements with his hands as if to show that they were safe and welcome. They were surprised to see that in spite of his superb body he was old — his grizzle of hair was nearly as white as wool. The electric light glared down unshaded and the water from their clothes dripped loudly in the stilly air which smelt of moisture.

A lift sighed at the end of the corridor, its gates rang, and the Chinaman came softly down the passage, still carrying the automatic. Nicky noticed that he had taken the long nail from his right forefinger, so they must have been detachable.

He said to the negro in a quiet tone, "Why?"

Then he went to Judy, turned her round to face

the other way and put the muzzle of the pistol against the base of her skull.

A voice on the loud-speaker system — for it seemed the place was wired for sound — said casually but slowly, "Waste not, want not."

The amplifier went click.

The Chinaman put away the pistol in a pocket inside his sleeve.

Nicky was sick.

Judy said furiously to the Chinaman, "What did you do that for?"

CHAPTER THREE

The Master

THEY woke in a kind of hospital ward with no windows. The walls and floor and even the ceiling were tiled with the same white, glazed tiles as the corridor had been. The beds were black iron. There were four empty ones as well as their own, with the grey blankets folded neatly on them. There was a trolley with thermometers and bandages and shining scissors. There were screens. In fact, it really was a hospital, and it had central heating.

The twins felt dopey.

"Nicky?"

"Yes?"

"Are you awake?"

"No."

"Please wake up."

He rolled about in a protesting way, snorting like a grampus, then said in a perfectly sensible voice, "How are you?"

"I'm hungry."

"My chin is sore underneath," said Nicky.

He considered this.

"I must have gone into the water feet first, so it hit my underneath sides, under my arms and under my chin and under my nose and under my eyelids and..."

He stopped to wriggle his toes, to find out about the soles of his feet, which had been protected by shoes.

"But *why?*"

"Why what?"

"Why did they push us off?"

"I suppose they didn't want us."

"Then why have they got us?"

"I don't know."

"They have got us, haven't they, Nicky?"

"Yes."

"Who are they?"

"I don't know."

After a bit, he asked, "Have you got anything on?"

She looked to see.

"Yes, a kind of night-shirt."

She added with pleased surprise, "It has tapes to tie round the middle."

"Mine has got *pockets*."

"So has mine."

"Well, that's something."

Later on, Nicky said, "Judy?"

"Yes?"

"I suppose these people live here."

"Yes."

"They must be hiding here."

"Yes."

"They didn't want us to find out."

33

"No."

"They pushed us off because they heard you say to fetch Daddy."

"Oh, Nicky!"

"You were quite right. We ought to have fetched him. It was my fault, Ju."

"Nick!"

He praised her about twice a year, so this was a glorious moment, even in their adversity.

"The Chinaman heard us from behind the door. They must have been listening."

"Then why did the black man save us?"

"Perhaps . . ."

"And what were they throwing?"

"The Chinaman was shooting at us."

"At us!"

"Oh, Judy, you are an ass."

He jumped out of bed and went to hug her, which twins sometimes feel like doing.

"And you did look so ridiculous getting ducked all the time."

"I am *not* ridiculous."

"You are."

"I'm *not*."

It was enchanting to be talked about, whatever he said, but there were sterner things to do than snuggle. They had to find out what was happening.

Nicky said, "Did you hear the Voice?"

"Yes."

"I believe that was the leader of them."

"Why?"

"Because when he said what he said, the Chinaman stopped doing what he was going to do."

"What was he going to do?"

"He was going to blow your head off."

She said in a small, pale voice, "As a matter of fact, I knew he was."

They were silent at this, two very unhappy children.

"Anyway, he didn't."

"No."

"Why did he say, 'Waste not, want not?'"

"Your head."

In a real flash of inspiration, he explained, "The Voice meant that we could be used for something."

"What?"

"I don't know. It meant that people are more useful alive than dead."

"Useful for what?"

"Useful for anything, I suppose."

Silence.

"I say, Nicky?"

"What?"

"I wish these night shirts weren't so big."

Silence.

"Nick?"

"Well?"

"The Chinaman is the second in command, and when their secret was going to be discovered he pushed us off the cliff, hoping it would kill us, but it didn't, so he shot at us in the water, and when Daddy found we were gone he would have thought we had tumbled off, and when the black man rescued us it must have been without orders or something, so the Chinaman came to finish us off and then the Voice stopped him and here we are."

"That's it."

"But oh," she wailed, "what *did* Daddy think? Where *is* Daddy? When will he come?"

Nicky felt even worse, but he put his arm round his sister and said, "He will come."

She shot up in bed.

"And where's Jokey?"

Not in that room.

Judy turned on her face, absolutely shattered, and sobbed into the pillow.

"The door is locked, Judy."

A sob.

"We are locked in."

Another.

"They will have Jokey downstairs somewhere. Perhaps they have a kennel."

"Jokey's dead."

Nicky suddenly went quite white, like your knuckles when you clench your fist, and said, "If Jokey is killed, I will kill them."

He went to the door and kicked it.

He said ragingly all he knew how to say, "Bloody, bloody, bloody!"

"You ought not to swear."

"Well, I did. And anyway, she's not."

"Not what?"

"Jokey is alive," he said, glaring at her as if she had defied him.

"Perhaps she is."

"Oh, Jokey!"

Later on, they grew more testy than miserable.

"Who are these people anyway?"

"Could they be pirates?"

"They don't have pirates nowadays, you ninny. At least, I don't think they do. Do they?"

"They have gangsters and smugglers."

"I don't see what you can smuggle in the middle of the Atlantic."

"Well, there must be *something* wrong", said Judy reasonably. "After all, they go about with pistols and push people off cliffs, which you would hardly do for a mother's meeting, would you?"

"Could they be spacemen or flying sorcerers or anything?"

"That's all rubbish."

"How do you know?"

"I know."

"Judy knows everything."

"Its kid's stuff — science fiction."

"Judy knows everything. Judy . . ."

They were on their way to a spat about this when the door opened silently, revealing a smiling man with a breakfast trolley.

He had a round, brown, bald face, twinkling with the fascination of his smile (false teeth). He announced in a fluting voice, "Good morning, kiddies. How's about some brekker?"

They looked at him aghast, for Kiddies and Brekker

were almost worse than Chinamen according to their
standards. With whiskers made of cotton wool he
could have been a first rate Santa Claus. He sounded
like a cuckoo, but seemed bent on being kind.

Judy said, in a society tone, "Do come in."

The false voice had made her feel false as well.

"Good morning."

"Good morning, my loves," he said. "Good morning, my pickaninnies. The top of the morning to ye,
says Bould Ben Backstay."

"Who?"

"Sure, 'tis only me, what they calls the ould Smiler."

Nicky ignored the introduction and demanded,
"Where is Jokey?"

"And who would Jokey be, might it plaze yer honour, when Jokey be's at home?"

"Where is our dog?"

"Ah, now, that's asking."

He said whitely, "Please tell me where she is at once."

"Aha!" said Bould Ben Backstay or Smiler or whoever he was. "Will ye listen now to me turkey cock!
Now here we haves some postie-toasties suited to the
juvenile appetites, and on the dish to de starboard is
iggs and bacon wit some of thim chipperlarters as
comes in tins. Indade, ye might say 'tis a faist for an
imperor ye have before ye, and all sairved up by gintle
Bonio, or Jacko de Peeper, as his messmates call him."

"Where is Jokey?"

"And dis does be de marmylaid."

"Our dog . . ."

"Now that's a crook question," said the gentle

Bonio, relapsing into Austrylian, and he bowed himself out backwards, softly rubbing his smooth hands,
with nods and becks and wreathèd smiles.

He locked the door.

"The beast!"

"Perhaps he was forbidden to tell us."

"Perhaps he didn't want to."

"If people kill your dogs, they say they have sold
them or given them away or sent them to a good home
or some foul lie like that."

"Don't talk about it, Judy. We don't know she's
dead. Perhaps the men in dungarees have got her.
Sailors and those sort of people are fond of pets. And
I know that on a liner you are not allowed to keep dogs
in your cabin, because they are looked after by the
butcher or somebody, down below."

"She'll be miserable."

"If we could get out of here," exclaimed Nicky. "I
bet the yacht is still there, looking for us. They
wouldn't go away without trying. There must be some
way of sending a message. If only there was a window!"

"Do you think we could bribe this Bonio or whatever he's called?"

"What with?"

"We could promise to make Daddy pay him."

"It would have to be Uncle Pierrepoint, because
Daddy hasn't any money."

"Uncle Pierrepoint could pay him in dollars. They
are valuable in England."

"We could try."

"We could tell him you are a Marquess, if that's any good."

After a bit, he said, "Ju, will you do the bribing? I don't think I know how to."

"Yes."

She was ruthless and would use any weapon, but he was shy about being a lord.

"We must offer to be ransomed.

"Kidnapped!" he added with satisfaction. "It's just like in Chicago. And sometimes they bump you off!"

But the bribery was a failure. When he brought their next meal, the kindly man only smiled like a pussy-cat. He refused to speak. Whatever they said, he smiled and smiled and was a villain.

The long afternoon was tedious, like being punished at school. They explored the boring, dead-white room, which would have been less inhuman if it had been cream — or any colour at all, for that matter, since white is not a colour. Judy noticed how the angles and corners were curved, to make sweeping easier, and her brother noticed the geometric exactness with which the tiles were cemented.

"I wonder how many rooms there are in this rock?"

"There were lots of rooms off those corridors."

"And a big lift."

"It must have taken ages to make."

"I could understand," added Nickey, "if they had blasted caves with dynamite or something, sort of rough like in a coal mine, but everything is done like a public lavatory. Pooh! That's just what it is like. But it must have taken millions of people to do it. There must be much more people than we saw."

"Do you think they could be making something here, like a factory? Perhaps they are forging something or boiling opium?'

"More likely atomic bombs."

"Could they?"

"I suppose not. You have to be as rich as a nation is to make them. As rich as Russia."

"Perhaps they are Russians."

"We haven't seen any so far."

"What is Bonio?"

"I don't think he's Irish really, do you?"

"He doesn't *look* unkind."

"He's beastly."

"You don't know he is. After all, he brought us our dinner."

"Oh, well, he's a steward or something. He has greasy hands."

"He can't help being a steward. Perhaps he's been washing up."

"Anyway, I don't like him. If he was decent he would tell us about Jokey."

"He may not know."

"Oh, all right."

After a gloomy pause, Judy said, "He may be a prisoner here, like us. Do you think they will keep us prisoners for ever?"

But the evening meal, when it came at last, did bring

something new to think about. It was a regular restaurant dinner, with tinned grouse which the children detested and an imitation pêche melba made from tinned peaches, and, of all things, a priceless claret to drink, which tasted like ink. It was served by Bonio, silent in a white jacket. His hands were trembling.

"What *are* you called?" asked Judy curiously.

He cleared his throat and answered in a hoarse voice. "Sure, it's what I tould ye. Little Nell."

"But you said you were Ben Backstay and then you said you were called the Smiler and . . ."

He went Scottish all of a sudden and whispered urgently, "Dinna tell him I convairsed wi' ye. Dinna let fall I spake one worrd."

"Tell who?"

He dropped a plate and said, "The Maister."

CHAPTER FOUR

Face to Face

H<small>E</small> took them down in the lift and along one of
the gleaming corridors, with its lights in the curved
ceiling, spaced like an underground railway station.
If you walked on the right-hand side of the tunnel,
each light made an arc on that side but not on the other,
like a perspective of comets or star-shells growing
smaller and smaller. It was a bit like the dazzle in a
gun-barrel. The corridor was muted with thick felt
matting. The silence of their footsteps and the un-
wavering stillness of the light gave them a feeling of
something waiting. They could hear the silence, or
feel it surging in their ears. In a way, it was obsequious
— like a very Grand Hotel.

At the end of the passage, there was a black ebony
door with heavy, discreet, eighteenth-century panels.
It was out of place, like a bit of Blenheim or Chats-
worth set down in an operating theatre. It glowed
with secrecy and opulence, saying, "Yes, in here."
Behind such doors, in ancient universities, the President's butler used to wait in white gloves, with a
silver tray for the visiting cards.

Bonio pulled one of those polished brass handles which tinkle bells in distant kitchens — bells on metal whorls like watch-springs, operated by wires.

The door opened of its own accord, in slow motion.

He signed to them to go in. He stayed outside. He was the colour of cheese.

In the old-fashioned hall, there were antlers — a twelve pointer — and a kind of umbrella-stand made from an elephant's foot with brass mountings. It had an alpenstock in it. There was an oil-painting by Landseer, showing a wise Newfoundland dog with its paw on a kitten, and a plaque underneath saying: *Stable Companions*. There was a mahogany hat rack with curly arms on which there hung a deerstalker hat and a plaid ulster. And yes, on the carved chest under the antlers, there was the silver salver for visiting cards with a pile of brown cards in it, weathered to the colour of tobacco. The top one said: *Mr. and Mrs. Charles Darwin.*

There were no doors out of this hall.

They went up a staircase with a worn Axminster carpet and found another door with bull-rushes painted on it. Some transfers of kingfishers were stuck on the rushes.

The second door opened and they went in.

The room was lit by paraffin lamps — what they used to call kerosene. They had pink silk shades with bows and flounces. The wallpaper was an intricate mixture of madonna lilies and tropical birds climbing on a trellis. There were Japanese fans on the walls and several paintings in heavy gilt frames — paintings in profile of ladies with copper hair and long, thick necks, mostly smelling sunflowers or kissing knights in armour. Water colours, in lighter frames, were of views at Zermatt, and there was a sepia photograph of the Colosseum in fumed oak. In one corner there was a container shaped like a drain pipe, made of papier-mâché, which was full of peacock's feathers, and in another corner the same sort of container with pampas grass.

The main feature of the room was an enormous custom-built radiogram, brand new.

They did not notice the furniture.

The Chinaman was in the room, standing silently in his dragon robe, half a pace to the right of another figure and half a pace behind it. His face had the unreadable look which Chinamen do have. The children did not see him.

It was the other.

He was dressed in a Norfolk jacket with cycling breeches and black stockings rolled into a kind of bangle below the knee. The high boots were protected by white spats. He was bald.

But he was as bald as an egg — worse, like a china egg — worse still, like cracklin china. For the skull and jowls and nose, and even the thin, yellow ears which you could almost see through, were traced with small lines or wrinkles, like millimetre graph paper which had wavered and set to the contours of the bone. If people keep their hands in the bath water for a long time, the fingers get puckered or wrinkled. This one's face had no wrinkles. The myriad lines were etched on it as if on ivory. They were as close together as pores, like the little sacks on the pig of an orange when you skin it. The surface was blotched here and there with brown stains, similar to freckles. Old billiard balls sometimes get to look the same as he did.

The hands were mottled.

He held out his right arm stiffly like a T-square, without turning round, and the Chinaman put a full glass of neat whisky in the claw.

He drank the whisky in three continuous gulps — held out the lizard hand again — rather like the tone-arm of an automatic gramophone changing the records — and dropped the glass, which did not break.

The Chinaman picked it up, refilled it, and put it back on the tone arm, which drained it without a pause.

Then he beckoned to Judy.

She went to the Master in a daze. He had blue eyes, as blue as sapphires, and with these, leaning forward slightly, he looked into hers. Strangely enough, considering his age, he did not wear spectacles. He looked for two minutes. Then, without anybody saying anything, Judy walked three or four steps backwards, as if leaving the presence of royalty, and the old man turned round to the dragon robe. He and the Chinaman put their foreheads close together in silence, almost touching, and remained like that for a minute. Then the Chinaman went out of the room.

Nicky was brave enough to say, "What are you doing to my sister?" Or rather, he was brave enough to try to say it, but the last part of the sentence was inclined to peter out.

There was no reply.

When the Chinaman came back, they stood still — or rather, all of them did but Nicky. He edged to his sister, watching them like a set of waxworks, ready to freeze if they moved. He whispered, "Judy?" She did not answer. He managed to get a view of her eyes. They were set. The pupils were enlarged like the brown eyes of horses. "Judy!"

Five minutes later there was a scratching on the door. It was opened from the outside by the shaky hand of Bonio.

Then what a pandemonium!

It was Jokey, covered with diesel oil, wildly hilarious, prancing among the peacock's feathers and pampas grass. Nicky dumped himself on his knees beside her for a hug, but she was too busy to attend to one person properly. She gave him a few sidelong licks in the face, as if to say, "Yes, yes: there, there: but let's do everything at once." Then she had wriggled free and was in the arms of Judy, who had wakened with the surprise. Next she was running round and round the room. In Judy's arms she wriggled to be off to Nicky, in Nicky's for Judy. She had no time to lick their noses before it was time to lick their ears. She panted while she licked and yapped while she panted. Even the Chinaman, watching the celebrations, almost smiled.

The Master halted the circus by raising his head from his breast — at which even Jokey, sensing the atmosphere, seemed to falter. This time it was Nicky who was beckoned to the presence.

He went resentfully, dragging his feet, scared, and raised his eyes to the blue ones against his will.

There was a long, seemingly endless look — two minutes, three, four, five.

The Master sighed. He seemed to take the air far down into his Norfolk jacket, his cycling breeches, his spats. He clicked his fingers, at which the Chinaman jumped as if he had been shot. He held out his arm, which was hastily provided with a third tumbler of whisky. He dropped the empty tumbler on the carpet.

Then, taking a deep breath, he said to Nicky in a voice of singular sweetness, "Non omnis moriar."

These were the only words spoken during the interview, except Nicky's.

CHAPTER FIVE

Hypnotized

Outside the black door, Bonio was in a dither. He had gone Cockney.

"Wot did e sye ter yer? Wotzee gonner do witcher?"

"He said something in Latin."

"Didjer unnerstan im?"

"It was Non Omnis Something-or-other."

"Latin, eye? That means eze pleased widjer. E speaks foreign when eze appy."

And suddenly, as they passed along the corridor, the dialects fell from Bonio, before he had got around to Welsh. From now till the last time they saw him he spoke like a stage clergyman, which was his natural tone. They never found out exactly why he had used the strange imitations to begin with. It might have been as a sort of disguise, or because he was by nature a deceiver, or perhaps it was a subtle way of teasing them. But now that they were in favour with the Master, and perhaps about to be important people in this queer group, none was so ready as Bonio to fawn upon them with the hand of Christian charity.

"My dear young friends," he said, "allow me to congratulate you on your success with our leader! A noble future lies before you, I have no doubt — a noble future as members of our happy band! Our happy band of brothers, I may say, upon this rock set in the silver sea, etc. Let your first friend be the first to share your triumph. Nothing, I repeat nothing, can be too much to do for youthful comrades, should it be only in my power. In any difficulty, apply to Dr. McTurk. Totty McTurk, they call me, on the lower deck — a form of nickname, you understand, common among the seafaring classes. You must regard me as a friend, nay, as a servant. Let us put it, as the servant of the servants of God, ha, ha. You can rely upon Totty absolutely. Although not privileged to enjoy the confidence of our Master like yourselves — for, depend upon it, if he has not only kept you but even spoken to you in Latin, there is a Purpose, yea, perhaps a mighty one — although not privileged to be chosen like yourselves — I am not without my uses, even I. A cog, my dears, a unit in the mighty scheme. Yes, even poor old Dr. McTurk was not found wanting. He is your friend. Rely on him. You may ask him anything, absolutely anything."

A demon of mischief rose in Nicky, as they listened to all this.

"Anything?"

"Anything."

"Then what's the square root of forty-nine million forty-two thousand and nine?"

Without batting an eyelid, Dr. McTurk replied at once, "Seven thousand and three."

Curled up in the hospital bed, with the oily mongrel nestling in her bosom, Judy said, "I thought he was *wonderful*."

There was no need to ask who.

"I don't see why."

"But Nicky, he was so *kind*. He was interested in everything I told him. He said he knew Daddy's great-grandfather. Gee, he must be old! That was after I had said who we were and how we came on Uncle Pierrepoint's yacht just to say we had been here and . . ."

"What are you talking about, Ju?"

"The Master of course. He couldn't have been nicer. And then when I told him how darling Jokey had been taken away and would be missing us he sent the Chinaman to fetch her and he said how he had had a Skye Terrier himself that was given to him by Queen Victoria called Rabbie and . . . "

"But, Judy, he didn't say anything to you at all!"

"Don't be silly. We talked for hours."

He gazed at her helplessly, doubting his senses.

"What did you tell him?"

"Everything. I told him how rich Uncle Pierre-point was and that he was a Senator in America, and he said he once knew a young man called Rockefeller who used to give dimes to golf caddies or something, and he said it would be nice to know Uncle Pierrepoint because he might be useful to him, and I told him about Mummy and he said he would send her a message that we were quite safe and he explained why we could not go back on the yacht just yet. . . ."

"Why not?"

"I can't remember."

"Why can't we go back on the yacht?"

"He explained, Nicky. You wouldn't understand. But he explained it beautifully and we are to stay here for a long holiday until he has got the thing done. . . ."

"What thing?"

"The thing he is doing. And then perhaps we can help him through Daddy — yes, he definitely said that, because of Daddy's connections or something — and then of course Jokey arrived and afterwards he began talking to you."

"He never talked to me."

"But I watched you. You were chatting for at least five minutes."

"I didn't say a single word."

"Nicky!"

"I didn't. I didn't. I didn't."

"Well, I wasn't listening, because I was playing with Jokey. But he must have said lots of things."

"He said exactly three words in Latin, and I didn't understand *them*."

"With all the conversation going on . . ."

Nicky sat up in bed and shouted, "It didn't happen! You're imagining it! You're mad! You're *hypnotized*!"

CHAPTER SIX

A Missing Tongue

THE yacht left on the second morning. The twins were let out of hospital when she was hull down.

It would be a mistake to think of them as helpless prisoners who needed pity.

For one thing, they had not lived long enough in the world to be sure of what was normal and what was not. They were better able to accept events than older people would be, and, like most children, they were cleverer than they seemed. Nor were they so heart-broken about being separated from their parents as parents would like to think. Judy had accepted the fact that they were there on holiday, and even Nicky — it is sad to confess — had been more worried about Jokey, who depended on him, than about his father, on whom he depended. They had the resilience of youth. They were surrounded by new things. They had puzzles to work out. The challenge to their adaptability was its own tonic.

They were not like Hamlet, who spent the time examining his own inside. They looked outwards, took matters as they came, and were inclined to do things first and think about them afterwards. In short, they scarcely glanced at the departing ship.

Or rather, Judy didn't. She wanted to find out about the rock.

It was different for Nicky, whose heart was heavier than hers was and who had more to puzzle out. Nothing he could say at breakfast would persuade her that she had not had a long conversation with the wizard, and this, for the first time in their lives, made a gap between them.

Besides, had she?

It was evident that the old man had sent for Jokey, whether they had talked about the dog or not.

There were other problems. How could Dr. McTurk have given the right square root of a figure in millions — for Nicky had worked it out — and why should these people be lurking on Rockall at all? What was the relationship between the different ones they had met? What did the Latin words mean?

He was not a fool. If it was true that the Master had talked with Judy somehow or other, by extra-sensory perception or something — and there was the queer way he had laid his forehead against the China-man's — then the "conversation" might really have happened. In that case, the old man had mentioned that Mr. Pierrepoint and the Duke could be useful to a plan. Could this be why they were being held?

On the other hand, he had seen for himself that not one word had passed between the Master and Judy. He remembered the strange look in her pupils. What was hypnotism anyway? How did it work? And if there had been some kind of thought transference, why had there been none with him?

The worst of it was that none of these problems could be discussed with his sister. Whatever the sapphire eyes had done, it lay between them. She got cross at once if anything were said against her new friend.

Nicky was the man of the two — he had the logical worries and the duty of protection.

Above all, what *was* the Master? How old was he, for instance? And why did Dr. McTurk seem terrified?

Anyway, they were loose. They had been told they could go wherever they liked, and exploring was one thing at least which they could still share.

Judy said, "I think we ought to go outside, in case Jokey wants to do her business."

The lift was big enough to carry a small truck and its top floor or landing was a brightly lighted workshop. The big room was empty in the middle, as if something was missing which ought to fit there, and round the walls there were work benches supplied with the machine tools of a good garage — lathes and electric welders and planing machines. There were spare parts in the shape of aerofoils, containers for fuel or lubricants, racks of spanners and screw-drivers and pliers and braces of every possible size, neatly matched. There was a bowser, looking like a big dor-beetle on small wheels. The cement in the middle was stained with droppings of oil like a bus station. At the far wall, running on overhead girders but folded back, was a heavy crane painted orange. Beyond the crane were the doors which they had seen from outside. It was made to swing through them.

The doors were counterpoised. After they had been unbolted, they opened to a gentle pressure.

The weather had changed for the worse, which was one of the reasons why the yacht had been forced to give up searching.

The silence and artificial light of the interior gave place to a great pounce of noise and dazzle as they stepped out on the ledge from which they had been pushed. The seabirds rose with a whirling of wings and a tumult of voices. The wind snatched at their night-shirts — now their only clothes — in which they looked like a pair of small Druids. The waves poised, paused, collected themselves with an outward suction, and heaved, hurled, hurtled upon the cliff-foot. Their plumes climbed into the sunny air with a woof, faltered at the zenith and tumbled back in streaming cataracts of white lace, tattered on the fangs of granite. That evening, an educated voice from the warm rooms of a radio station would be using the familiar phrases about "Rockall, Malin, Hebrides" with the forecast about "reaching gale force at times". It would be a far voice in every sense from the captured twins.

They withdrew to the garage as soon as the dog was ready, for fear she might be blown away. Jokey, with her hair swept over her head like the White Queen's in Alice, kicked backwards industriously, to show that she had finished.

The lift took them down to the next floor, which

was empty like the top one. It was a recreation room, as big as the one above it. There were two billiard tables, dart boards, a shove-ha'penny board beautifully polished with no beer-rings on it, and a skittle alley — the English kind in which wooden cheeses are thrown, not rolled. Leather settees stood round the walls with buttons to stitch their upholstery, like the buttons in an old-fashioned railway carriage. On the walls themselves, there was the rather touching bric-à-brac which seamen and people in barracks seem to collect — pictures of Diana Dors cut out of magazines, detailed cover illustrations from the *Saturday Evening Post* by Rockwell or Hughes, views of celebrated objects such as the Eiffel Tower, cheering thoughts by Patience Strong snipped from the *Daily Mirror* — such as,

> *Though the sorrows of bereavement linger in the*
> *mind,*
> *Happy is the memory that you have left behind*

—and photographs of horses being kind to kittens or dogs sharing dishes of food with canaries. These were mixed up with printed notices about fire-alarms and life jackets. There was a notice board which said there would be a smoking concert last Friday, also the usual billiard markers and a couple of chalky slates with numbers written up. One of them had a rough picture of a scrubbing brush drawn at the bottom.

The next floor downwards was bigger. It was divided into cubicles with bunks in tiers and a wash-house with sea-water showers and basins at one end. There were enough bunks for at least fifty people, but only six of the cubicles seemed to be in use. The blankets in the empty ones were folded away. There were no pin-ups on their walls. The bedside chairs were upside down on the blankets.

The used cubicles had tables next to the bunks, with hobbies spread on them — a ship being put in a bottle, a lobster pot being woven, a collection of shopping bags being netted out of string, a fretwork pipe-rack, a cushion cover beautifully embroidered with humming birds, a dozen cigar boxes decorated with glued feathers in fancy patterns.

"Where *is* everybody?" asked Judy.

The next landing had the usual tiled corridors going to the four points of the compass. The lower the lift went, the more space there was, because the rock was narrower at the top. Some of the rooms must have been below sea level.

The passages had doors with names on them. There was their own door (HOSPITAL), next to CHIEF ENGINEER, STEWARD, DARK ROOM, S/LDR. FRINTON, SURGERY, ACCOUNTS. One of the passages was taken up with STORES, KITCHEN, MESS DECK, and another was devoted to various offices. The fourth passage led to the ebony door. The Master's quarters were on the other side of its blank wall.

The lowest floor and the biggest had people in it at last. On one side of the lift there was the passage leading to the ebony door, on another side the one leading to the casement by which they had entered — but the other side stood in a great engine room like the bowels of a liner, in which the men in dungarees moved

about their business. It would need a qualified
engineer to explain the wonders of this workshop and
mass of machinery — the power plant, the heating
system, the air conditioner, the lighting and the
rest.

But it was domestic. Nothing was being made there,
so far as they could see, except the needs of life.

The men in jeans were pleased to meet the twins
and enjoyed patting Jokey. They showed off their
dials and gauges with honest pride — keeping the dog
away from moving parts — and answered technical
questions from Nicky without reserve.

Yes, they said, the main problem was drinking
water, which had to be brought by sea in the trawler
and pumped into these here tanks under the floor.
They insisted on lifting the man-holes to show the
water supply — the dank humidity of lightless water
underfoot. And yes, the twins would see the trawler
in a day or two, when she paid her next visit. No,
they explained, there were no more people living
on the rock than themselves. Sometimes the crew of
the trawler slept there for a night or two — or some of
them did — but the tiers of bunks in the forecastle
were a left-over from the time the island was hollowed,
which was long ago. The workmen had gone now,
nobody knew where. They were mostly Italians.

No, they said laughing, they were not making hydro-
gen bombs — just maintenance, that was all they were.

What were they maintaining? Well, they were
working for the Master.

Nicky noticed that, although they liked answering

questions about their engines, they began to look vague
on wider subjects. Their eyes grew horse-like, just as
Judy's had done the night before, and the replies were
duller the further you went, till they became blank with
silence. The men were not hiding anything. They
simply did not know — were not interested — and
seemed even to forget the questions while they were
being put. It was like water off a duck's back.

All he could gather was that the Chinaman and Dr.
McTurk and the negro — whose name was Pinky —
and the squadron-leader, whose name they had seen
on a door, were the experts helping with the Plan.
What plan? The answer was a stare.

Except for this deadened place in their minds,
which was as dumb as novocaine might make it, the
men in jeans were normal — like lighthouse keepers,
whom they resembled. Lighthouse keepers are inclined
to dislike one another, being cooped up together, so
that they grow silent and attend to their own hobbies,
but apart from the slight tension of knowing each other
too well the engineers were tranquil. They were even
cheerful for the time being, since Jokey and the twins
were a novelty for them — giving them something new
to think about. One of the men had actually kept a
bone for Jokey, which he presented shyly, and which
Jokey accepted out of politeness but hid behind a
transformer.

"Who stole Jokey?" asked Judy, remembering
about this.

They did not know.

They were grieved to hear she had been stolen.

They had only seen her when she was rescued from the sea.

A rather pathetic thing was the way they made up to the little dog and envied the one who had thought of the bone. Perhaps all men want to have something to look after, even if it is only a wife, and this may be the reason why sailors are always turning up with parrots in cages or ship's cats or green-furred mona monkeys who generally die on passage.

Judy was not particularly interested in pressure gauges, and most of Nicky's questions were out of keeping with her mood. They grated on her. She knew what the Master's plan was — although she had forgotten its nature so that she could not exactly explain. The questions seemed suspicious to her, if not bad manners. After a time, she exclaimed impatiently, "Let's go and see the kitchen."

On the way up in the lift, Nicky made a last attempt.

"What *is* the plan, Judy?"

"You were rude," was all she said.

"But why didn't they know about it?"

"I suppose they were hypnotized," she said sarcastically, "like me."

"Please, Judy."

"Oh, shut up. Shut up, shut up, shut up!"

And she began dancing about in the cage of the lift, chanting these words in a way which she knew infuriated him.

The kitchen was almost as technical as the engine room. Its deep-freeze and refrigerators and electric whisks and washing machines and potato peelers and tin-openers which wound with handles were not common objects in England, even in a ducal mansion visited by the public at two shillings and sixpence a time — guide book extra. The housewife in Judy was enchanted. "Oh!" she exclaimed. "Look, cardboard cups you can throw away!"

The occupant of the kitchen was the negro, Pinky, and he was as delighted as Judy was, to receive a visit. Although the men had said that he was one of the higher technicians, he was the cook as well. He took them round in a delicious whiff of vegetable soup, and onions being slowly cooked golden with the lid on.

Jokey got a steak done from inside by radiation in two minutes, which she ate voraciously, while the huge black man grinned all over his face and snapped his fingers.

Nicky tried him with questions when he saw that his sister was poking about the bread ovens.

The man smiled and nodded and twinkled his treacle-coloured eyes, but answered nothing.

Finally he opened his mouth like a great codfish, or like lifting the lid of a piano keyboard, and held it for the boy to see.

There was no tongue in it.

CHAPTER SEVEN

The Sum of the Evidence

THE trawler turned up three days later. She was an ordinary fishing boat, trawling the submarine bank on which Rockall lay, and she did fish. When she went back to Northern Ireland after her trip, her holds were filled with a real catch. Nobody suspected or asked her what had happened to the cargo she delivered. Her crew was as blank on the subject as the engine-room staff had been. They thought of themselves as fishermen. Their eyes had the horse look if you mentioned anything else. They did not know that they were hiding anything.

This gave Nicky a feeling of relief. He had been brooding at night — for Judy refused to discuss it — about the fate of the Italians who had hollowed out the island.

He had heard that when people hide things of value in secret rooms, with the help of masons and carpenters, they usually execute them afterwards, for fear they should blab. He knew that oriental potentates, wicked barons in the early Middle Ages and all successful Borgias in general — pirates too — did this. He shared

63

no part of his sister's reverence for the Master — incidentally, everybody seemed to share it except Dr. McTurk and perhaps Pinky — and in the constrained darkness of the hospital room at night he had worried about those fifty men. His own view of the Master was that he was capable of killing the lot — yes, and able to, for it was obvious that he had power.

It was a relief to think that they might have been sent back to Italy with blank minds, like the trawler-men and the engineers.

The trawler's visit left one more person to be met. He arrived out of a rain-storm, making the tremendous racket which helicopters do make, and his aircraft was hauled into the top garage, now seen to be a hanger, by the crane. It was fitted with cylindrical floats, each like a metal Li-Lo. Its rotors had to be taken down before it was hoisted. S/Ldr. Frinton, wearing a wet bowler hat and dusting the raindrops off his town coat, supervised the work.

He was a strong, square-set man of middle height with a dense black beard cut like Lenin's. He was about thirty-five years old, but was going bald. When he took off his bowler, he put on a stocking cap to keep his head warm. He had red lips and looked ferocious in repose, but when he smiled it was with a tender expression, like the Master's voice. He did smile, for Pinky was there to meet him, patting his hands together with pleasure. He said, "Hi, Pinky! How's the blackamoor?" He was pleasant to the engineers who stowed the helicopter. He had the presiding courtesy which used to be a feature of the Royal Air

Force. He noticed the twins with surprise, but shelved them with a not unfriendly nod because he was busy — or perhaps puzzled. When the aircraft was housed, he sank down in the lift, intent on something else. He seemed a dynamic, preoccupied man. Nicky had taken an instant dislike to him.

This completed the inhabitants of Rockall and was the sum total of evidence open to the prisoners, even if Judy refused to admit that she was one.

It was the puzzle — evidently a dangerous puzzle, when you remembered the cliff and the pistol — which the boy had to solve.

Nicky lay in the hospital bed that evening with his eyes fixed on the electric bulb. There was a dim blue one for the night time, which was not switched off till twelve o'clock. They were no longer locked in.

He lay on his back in the eerie light, mulling it over, absent-mindedly sucking a button which had come off his nightshirt. It crossed his mind that it was a nuisance having nothing else to wear, and still more of a nuisance having no shoes. Both children had lost theirs, torn off by the crash in the sea, so that they had to patter about in bare feet. The costume was fine for the summer, but suppose they were kept till colder weather? There would be nothing to fit them in the island. Perhaps the helicopter would bring something. Luckily, the stores had plenty of toothbrushes and combs. He must ask for some blue jeans to be cut down. Perhaps Judy could sew them. Perhaps. . . .

His fair hair looked greenish in the bulb's cold glow, and his thin, sunburned hands, now looking grey, fiddled and fiddled with the place where the button used to be.

Elsewhere, the islanders pursued their own mysterious concerns.

The engineers were distributed between the engine room, the recreation room and the dormitory. The two who were on duty moved in the quiet whine of the generators, absently wiping their hands on oily rags and glancing at the arrows of pressure gauges which sometimes just perceptibly vibrated with life but lay most of the time as still as crocodiles on a sand bank, pointing in different directions — or perhaps like minnows drowsing in a still pool, for they were prickly like minnows. Two others were playing shove-ha'penny, upstairs, in solemn silence. They had the rigid morals of first-rate players and would not dream of claiming a coin unless it was actually in the middle of a bed. Even if it was slightly nearer one line than the other, without touching, they ignored it loftily. They had no scorer and did not score for each other. The shover either did or did not mark his own chalks and there was neither protest nor discussion. The last two were in the dormitory, sharing a pot of glue. The glue, which had to be heated on a spirit stove, was a link between them, so that they spoke to each other sometimes. The one with the ship in a bottle was pulling its masts upright, already rigged, and the feather man was quickly and neatly applying a mosaic of matched Guillemot plumage — a dark brown rather like the blotches on their eggs. He used the delicate pliers which electricians have.

Pinky, alone in his own workshop which had once been the dark-room, was also doing delicate work. His long, spatulate, black fingers, almost rosy inside, flashed neatly every now and then from one watchmaker's tool to another, in the pool of light thrown by a reading-lamp. He wore an eyeshade and the glass which jewellers screw into one eye. There was a blueprint tacked to the wall in front of him, with only its lower half lighted by the zone of the lamp. His mouth was open. If he had been a child and if he had had a tongue, it would have been stuck out. He was making a machine or instrument not unlike a tiny scanner for radar, except that it was inside out. A completed one stood on the table in front of him.

Dr. McTurk was in his cabin, under a similar reading lamp. It had a standing desk like an architect's, with a blotter on it which could be pushed across what he was writing. The blotter was already laid out with various sheets of calculations which he might seem to be making, but the real calculations would be underneath when he pulled it over them. His round face looked furtive, greedy and tired — no longer benevolent — and he was doing something which was silly. He was trying to work out accurate great-circle measurments on an ordinary school atlas from the island's library. Apart from his special work, he did not seem to be an intelligent man. While he worked, you could almost see his ears pricked.

When the door opened without knocking, and the

Chinaman came swiftly in, the blotter was as swiftly pulled across the atlas — in fact, more swiftly. It slid across with the bland dexterity of a conjuring trick or a card sharper dealing, and Dr. McTurk was all urbanity and deference. He took the list of equations from his silent visitor, looked them over casually and gave the answers. The Chinaman wrote them down and bowed. The doctor bowed. The door closed behind the Chinaman, and McTurk, turning back to the architect's desk, noticed that the right side of his upper lip above the canine tooth was fluttering. He could not stop it. It tickled.

S/Ldr. Frinton was another of the lonely ones under a single light. He was writing in a large, round hand, very fast, with bad punctuation. His education in the second world war had not been scholastic.

He was writing his Will.

The Chinaman lifted his arm high and took hold of the stag's antler. He pulled it downwards. The wall, with the antlers and the chest and the tray of visiting cards, swung in like the breech-block on a naval gun, showing the laboratory beyond them, ablaze with light.

The great room was as sterile as a morgue, but not as empty and not as silent. It had noise and light and movement. A hum played background to a whine — generators and transformers. The cathode-ray valves glowed with a green fluorescence, while the rectifiers had a purple fire, due to the mercury. Oscillators twinkled as they caught the highlight, going click, click, click, like a rapid metronome. The iconoscope stood big and square and solid, emphasizing the steady secrecy of sound and motion — which were themselves a kind of silence because they were regular — like the throb of your blood in your ears. Absolute silence can be heard and seen.

The far wall of the laboratory was hung with maps and charts, more accurate than poor McTurk's had been. There were even maps of the air, in plan and elevation, with Heaviside layers and currents of high-altitude winds. The inner walls had thousands of books.

An unexpected thing at the far end was a set of chessmen half-way through a game, standing on what looked like an operating table. The Master was standing beside them, as motionless as they were.

The Chinaman put McTurk's list of figures on a spike like a bill file and went to the table. He moved a bishop six paces along its diagonal. The Master's tone arm came out smoothly and castled the black king.

CHAPTER EIGHT

Conspirators

"Ju?"

"Yes?"

"Perhaps he really did talk to you," he said with a gulp, not being used to being in the wrong. "You know — he might have — sort of by reading minds?"

"He talked," she said flatly.

"You might give in a bit."

She was almost out of her sulks, so she said suspiciously, "I will if you will."

"Then he did talk."

"Honest?"

"Honest."

"Oh, Nicky, then perhaps he did too."

"Did what?"

"Read minds. But it doesn't matter. So long as we explained to each other it doesn't matter how, does it? I don't know what you are making such a fuss about, Nicky. Why are you so horrid to him?"

"If he explained, how did he explain?"

"It's difficult."

"Did he say what they are making or planning or whatever it is?"

70

"Yes."

"Well, what?"

"He said it was all right."

"Judy, *what*?"

Perhaps — because they were twins — his mind was closer to hers and had more influence over it than ordinary people would have. Perhaps, in contact with her brother, she was less far gone than the trawlermen and the engineers had been. She began tying and untying the tapes round her waist nervously, looking distressed. He went over to her bed in the blue light and sat beside her, scratching Jokey.

"Please, dear Judy."

She said with difficulty, "I don't know what he explained."

"Don't you see that it can't be all right if they shoot at people?"

"Perhaps it was a mistake. Yes, it was. He said it was."

"People don't make mistakes like that. And if it is a holiday, why didn't Mummy and Daddy come and say good-bye to us? Why were we locked up?"

She began to cry.

"Never mind, Ju. We will think another time."

"No."

"No what?"

"I will think now."

He sat absolutely still, holding his breath. Jiminy, he thought, I believe I've brought her round. Wait.

She said, "I don't know what he said. It's fuzzy. I believe . . . Did you feel sleepy?"

"It never worked on me at all."

"What didn't?"

"What he was doing with his eyes or his brain or whatever it was."

"But he did speak to you?"

"He spoke to me in Latin because he was pleased it didn't work. What's more, he had to have another tumbler of whisky before he could say it. I don't believe he *can* talk without the whisky, not like us. He talks with his eyes or his forehead or something."

"Ants do," said Judy conversationally, in her normal tone. "They put their antennae together. It says so in Biology."

"And that is what he did to you."

"Nick, how thrilling! It means I can talk like ants and you can't."

"It also means that he can read whatever you are thinking, and that he can make you think whatever he wants."

"That's what he's done to the engineers."

"Yes."

"How horrible!"

"He could make you think you were a sausage," said Nicky, pursuing his advantage.

"He couldn't."

"He could."

"But sausages can't think."

He opened his mouth and shut it again.

"If . . ."

"Nicky, would he know if I wanted to go to the place?"

"Certainly."

"Beastly! He would . . . I believe he *did* hypnotize me and its nastier than anything."

"So you see."

She did see, or rather, she was willing to.

"If this man . . ."

He stopped. He wanted to call him "This man", with all his ducal blood. But he could not. It was false. He remembered the eyes as he spoke.

"If the Master" he said, and they both glanced at the door, "if the Master . . ."

They were silent in the stagey light, watching the door handle.

When they began again, it was in whispers.

"We have *got* to do something. We have *got* to find out. We shall never get back to Daddy unless we do. Obviously that flying man and the Doctor and Pinky are working for them, for Him and the Chinaman I mean, and we must know what. It is something tremendous, Judy, and it's wrong."

"How can we find out?"

"We shall have to investigate."

The four syllables cheered him up, so he added, "We shall have to screen them."

"I don't think we quite ought to do that."

"It's like what the F.B.I. does to people."

"Oh, I see."

Not being sure what the F.B.I. was, she was forced to see.

"The point is that until we know *what* they are

doing and *who* they are, we can't do anything about it."

"No."

"So we must spy on them."

"Do you think you could?" she asked doubtfully, with more insight into Nicky than he knew.

"How do you mean?"

"Well . . ."

After thinking, she put it as kindly as she was able.

"I don't think spies are like Red Indians."

He was annoyed by the implied criticism.

"I . . ."

"It isn't like promising people not to tell things or listening at keyholes, Nicky. I think it's more like not knowing what you are doing yourself."

"We could listen at keyholes."

"Well," she said, relieved that it was to be not serious, more like a game, "I suppose we could."

"We could follow them about."

"Shadow them."

"Exactly."

"It won't be very easy shadowing people in a tiled corridor."

"We could search their rooms," he said uneasily, "when they are not there."

The more practical their remarks, the more they lowered their voices.

"If they caught us?"

He did not know what would happen then, as it was outside his experience. Spies are clearly not spanked or sent to bed — not in a world where people shoot with pistols. He did realize, and so did Judy, that it was silly for two twelve-year-olds to set about foiling great conspiracies.

But he knew they were right, all the same.

For one thing, they were in a real position, which forced them to behave in a certain way of its own accord. For another thing, he was sure that he could deceive when he wanted to. Children are expert liars if they trouble to forget the truth. Also, he knew that he was nimbler than adults are and that they would both be safer because they were children. It is an advantage to be thought childish and simple (though he did not realize this) when you are going to be a spy.

They became quite reasonable, and, not looking at one another, said under their breaths:

"This room may be wired for sound."

"Every room may be."

"The first thing is to find out about people."

"We can wander round."

"Read anything you find."

"Ask questions."

"Think."

He lay on the bed with his mouth against her ear and breathed as if to his own soul, "Not to begin with the Master. Begin with the easier ones."

She moved her head stealthily, as if they were watched, until her mouth was at his ear.

"Begin with Pinky."

"Why?"

"I think he is kind."

"How?"

75

"Just make friends."

Back in his own bed, Nicky was warm and happy to have got back his sister. But a bad thought struck him before he went to sleep. Suppose the Master could do whatever it was again — whenever he sent for her?

CHAPTER NINE

The Doctor

"What's the good of talking to Pinky if he's dumb?"

"Perhaps he can write."

"Whizzo!"

However, it turned out that the negro was inclined to be simple in his head.

He understood about fine machinery — perhaps he was one of the best watch-makers in the world, and that may have been why he was being kept on Rockall — but he seemed to have no views beyond what a child's might be. Judy had been right about him being kind.

"Pinky, why have you got no tongue?"

He wrote on a slate, in the copy-book handwriting of long ago, slanting and beautiful: "Gone."

They did not like to ask if anybody had done it to him.

"What are you making?"

He showed them the small, convex scanners proudly, but he had no idea what they were for.

"Who is Squadron-Leader Frinton?"

Some kind of dread prevented them from putting more important questions.

77

He wrote: "Good."

Judy asked on the spur of the moment, "Who stole Jokey?"

He knew, because the thief had had to apply for dog food at the kitchen. He wrote with the squeaky chalk, "Doctor."

And the Doctor came in as if on cue.

"Aha!" said he, looking at the slate before he looked at anything else. "Talk of an angel and we hear the rustling of his wings! Good morning, good morning, good morning. And why have our detectives been taking the medical name in vain? No, no, don't answer it. A joke, I assure you. No criticism intended. Every friend of Totty McTurk is welcome to talk about him to his heart's content, indeed it is an honour to which he is more than sensible — or is it sensitive? Dear me, now I wonder what the flattering question could have been?"

Nicky said without ado, "We were asking why you stole Jokey."

He was upset. He was wounded. He cast about for something to ease his sorrow, spreading his hands.

"My dears, I must explain. We must get together. There must be no misunderstanding between pals."

"Then why?"

"It is a lovely day," said the Doctor. "Let us betake ourselves to God's own sunlight, and thrash this complicated matter out."

It was not a lovely day. They stepped from the hangar doors into a dense fog, like pearls dissolved in skimmed milk. Its condensation hung on the granite.

The Doctor

It was so thick that it acted like something solid, returning an echo to their voices and making their footsteps hollow or cavernous. Even bare feet made a reverberation. The birds of the cliff-top did not rise when the doors opened. They could not afford to. They sat where they were, tamed silly by the element. When there is no hope, there is no fear, and there was no hope now of flying.

"What's the good of going out in this? We'll get soaked."

"Fall off, more likely."

"Hold Jokey."

"Jokey! Jokey! Come here, darling. You'll tumble off."

"I *hate* Jokey on cliffs," added Judy. "I know they're supposed to be sure-footed and all that, but how can you be certain? Besides, she's a born idiot, aren't you, sweetheart?"

"Good Doggie," said the Doctor. "Poor Doggie."

This sealed his damnation so far as they were concerned. Nobody calls dogs Doggie.

"Well?"

"As your little sister has mentioned so sensibly, perhaps we had better go in again before we get wet."

He stood doubtfully in the hangar, not knowing where to take them. He had wanted to be out of doors because, like them, he was afraid of microphones. The sound system was one of the secrets which he had not fathomed. But he wanted to talk.

"My surgery?"

The room was not so well equipped as the other

technical places had been. It was in a muddle. A side table was crowded with serums and ampoules and bottles with the wrong cork in, diphtheria cheek by jowl with penicillin, and there were broken needles for hypodermics and the thing they hold your tongue down with was rusty. The twins sat side by side on the black leather couch, Judy noticing with distaste that an enamel bin still had stale bits of bloody lint in it, mixed with cigarette ends.

"Well?"

He started on a deep breath.

"It was essential to take you away from the negro, children. I had to get you out of there."

They examined the statement without belief.

"He is mad," explained the doctor.

Judy thought, Well, he does seem a bit simple. Do mad people behave like that? The Doctor saw what she was thinking. "No, no, he is worse than simple. He gives you that impression because of his good nature. But he is deluded — genuinely insane. You must be careful about being alone with him, and above all you must not rely on anything he says. I should say, writes. We call it delusional insanity in the profession. You must take the word of a medical man, children — believe me you must — or you may be in great danger. Poor fellow! That is why we keep him here on the rock — a kind of sanatorium for him. Gentle as a lamb most of the time, obliging, the soul of kindness — although his ideas are quite disordered. And then, suddenly, Pouf! Manic-Depressive. You can't believe a word he says."

"He said you had taken Jokey."

"Exactly. I had to get you away. Thwart him for a moment — contradict one of his notions — and there you are in the middle of a crisis. It would have been dangerous even to deny such an idea in front of Pinky."

"Did you take her?"

The Doctor twinkled all over his fat face.

"Really!"

For that matter, there did not seem to be any particular reason why he should.

"Why did you put on all those different voices when we were locked up?"

His hurt look was almost dignified.

"My sense of humour," he said, blowing his nose. "We are not accustomed to children on the island. You must forgive it. A mistaken friend."

"Why are we here?"

"And what," added Judy, "is everybody doing? Unless you tell us, we can't trust anything, not for true."

"That is what I wanted to talk about. Wait a minute, I believe I have some ju-jubes."

He scrabbled about in a drawer and brought out some cough-drops or pastilles in a soiled paper bag, which the twins accepted reluctantly. They were black and tasted of a mixture of liquorice and currants.

"I must tell you from the beginning. We must lower our voices. Pull the couch to this corner here, where it is further from the door.

"Now, children," began the Doctor. "No doubt you have heard of Top Secrets. You know — things that can only be mentioned in the Cabinet, if there. Sir Winston Churchill even, could only allow himself to discuss them on a scrambled telephone. Well, that is what we are working on at Rockall. I hardly know whether I ought to speak about the matter, even to you!"

"If it is a secret," said Nicky, "don't tell us."

"I am compelled by circumstances — that's it, compelled by circumstances. Your arrival here — the accident of your purely fortuitous arrival, I might say, forces me to reveal the truth."

He thought this over and added, "You realize that we tried to destroy you? A hideous choice, kiddies, but one which had to be taken. When the lives of millions are in the balance, the lives of two must be discounted. That's the scientific attitude."

"We know that we didn't exactly shoot at ourselves."

"Yes. Yes. Ahem! Well, you must learn the truth, the whole truth and nothing but the truth. Then you can judge of the dilemma."

His voice sank to an inaudible squeak, recovered itself and became a whisper. He leaned forward and said, "*We are working against the H-bomb.*"

They waited.

"Deterrence," said the Doctor, "or Defence. You will have heard the arguments. Either you can deter the enemy by making more and better bombs, or you can invent a counter-weapon which renders them harmless. Renders the bombs, I mean. That is what we are doing here."

In the impressive pause which followed, Nicky asked, "Do *you* know about atoms?"

"No. Well, no. I am the physician, the humble minister who keeps the greater brains — I might say, the irreplaceable souls — in health and fitness. That is what I shall have to tell you about."

They waited again.

Dr. McTurk transferred a dusty thermometer, which had been lying in a kidney dish, into a glass of water which had a spare set of false teeth in it.

"Mine is a difficult task."

He noticed, without registering the fact, that the bulb was broken off the thermometer.

"The mind," he exclaimed. "The human mind — that is the difficulty. These tremendous thinkers whose vast brains are beyond the ken of simple folk, they are inclined — inevitably inclined — to be abnormal, neurotic. It is the *sanity* of the Master which I have to guard, as a medical man, rather than his physical health. The one reacts upon the other.

"My dear children, you can scarcely imagine the difficulties which confront me. You lack the training in medical psychology."

He took the thermometer out of the glass and threw it in the bin for used lint.

"I will try to explain in simple terms. If the Master is ill, he thinks badly. If he thinks badly, he gets ill. You understand?"

They nodded.

"And if he is thinking badly, he will not trust his own physician."

After this had partly sunk in, he went on, "It is essential for a doctor to follow the workings of the brain.

"Diagnosis," he cried, giving the table quite a thump, "is impossible if the symptoms are concealed. The Master is a sick man. He will not confide in me. He refuses to take my medicines. I am powerless to aid, nay, to protect, the most important secret in the world!"

The fist which had struck the table straightened out and became a flat hand on it. The red vanished from his face, which changed on the instant to a coaxing smile. He looked as innocent as a baby.

"You could help."

"How?"

"By telling me about your interview."

There seemed to be an unwillingness to do this, so he explained still further.

"Everything the Master says or does, every action of the patient and his mental processes, everything is relevant to his state of health — a health beyond price to suffering humanity."

"Who is the Master?"

"The greatest scientist alive."

"If," began Nicky, but Judy trod on his toe.

She said, "Well, we only talked about personal matters really. He mesmerized me, but he couldn't do it to Nicky."

The Doctor was radiant for one blink of a second, like a light switched on and off.

"How much did he drink?"

84

"Three glasses."

"Three!"

"And he had to speak to Nicky because he couldn't read his mind."

"I knew it! I knew! This is the fourth time it has happened."

"The fourth of what?"

"Never mind," he said — then, remembering his kindness, "Professional secrets, dears. The oath of Aesculapius. Doctors must never tell about their patients, must they, as you are old enough to understand?"

He thought for a minute, looking at the floor. When he looked up his face was tired.

"You will be willing to help old Totty?"

At their silence, he added with pathos, "It is the fate of the world."

"All right," said Judy, before Nick could say anything.

"I want you to do two things. Listen carefully and remember. By the way, what were your names?"

"Nicky and Judy."

"I want you, Nicky, to see as much as you can of the Master. Make friends with him. He will begin to have you educated now, so you will be seeing him like that. Remember what he says and does, and tell me all about it. And you, Judy, I don't want you to see him at all — if you can help it. He will not be educating you, so it ought not to be difficult. You do realize that everything is in the interests of the patient?"

"Yes."

"To establish a contact with the patient's mind?"

"Yes."

"There's a pair of clever children! You will do it for Totty's sake as well as for the safety of the world?"

"We will do our best," said Judy, meaning it, "to do what's right."

"Spoken like a Britisher!"

They were loathing this description of them when he changed the subject.

"Well, well. So much for that. And now I must get on with my dispensing."

He winked at the children cheerfully, even briskly.

"Medicine," he explained, "a ministering angel thou! Dispensing, dispensing, dispensing. A bottle here and a bottle there. Who knows — perhaps even a sedative for our honoured Master?"

They were shutting the door when he called them back.

"You have heard of the Official Secrets Act?"

"Yes."

"Not one word to one single soul — you understand clearly?"

"Yes."

"Not to Pinky, not to Frinton, not to the Chinaman, not even to the Master?"

"No."

"Don't forget it," he said. "This is not a game of Let's Pretend."

When they were safe in their own room, Nicky asked mildly, "Did you believe any of that?"

"Not much. He doesn't even clean his finger-nails."

CHAPTER TEN

Judy Thinks It Out

Bᴜᴛ he was right about the education. Before they could investigate Frinton or anybody else, the Chinaman opened the hospital door and beckoned to Nicky, the same day after dinner. He bowed to Judy as they left and said, "You will excuse us?"

Most Chinaman are supposed not to be able to pronounce their "r's", so that they say Flied Lice for Fried Rice. This one was not like that. He had a faultless accent. It was the real old-fashioned English kind — in fact, it was Edwardian. He would have said Umour instead of Humour, as the upper classes in those days did, if he had troubled to use the word at all.

Nicky followed him down the corridor.

They passed the black door and the antlers, the Axminster carpet and the door with bull-rushes.

In the Master's boudoir — for that was one of the few words which could describe its greenery-yallery ornaments — or perhaps it was more like the bachelor rooms of Sherlock Holmes in foggy Baker Street, among the Hansom Cabs — in the Master's boudoir, an inlaid writing desk had been carefully arranged with clean blotting paper, an ink pot and a steel pen with a relief nib. There was a typed examination paper on the blotter.

Good Heavens, thought Nicky, just like the Entrance Examination for Eton!

It was. There they were, the whole dreary rout of them: questions about equations, diagrams of right-angled triangles, etc., with their miserable points called A, B, C and D, inquisitions into the products of Chicago or the capital of Siam, dates of the French Revolution and a bit of *De Bello Gallico* to translate — the lot. Caesar! What made the whole thing even more unreal — or perhaps, for Nicky, real, since examinations had been more a part of his life till then than gangsters had been — the Chinaman was there to invigilate.

He sat down miserably at the writing desk, while the guinea-coloured man, his hands tucked in the wide sleeves, went into a standing trance.

Why doesn't anybody talk, thought the boy angrily, as he picked up the pen? Why these mysterious silences? Why all the hou-ha? You would think they could say Good morning or something. And he wrote down 1066 for the discovery of America, on purpose.

It was a kind of General Knowledge Paper.

How could they, how *could* they, shoot at you one day and give you a General Knowledge Paper the next? It was like a Mad Hatter's Tea Party.

Sitting on the hospital bed by herself, with a handful of Jokey's hair clutched too tightly in a furious fist —

Jokey bore it patiently, knowing that she was helping in the crisis — Judy was pondering the hideous unfairness of a woman's fate.

First of all, your brother got the title. Second, you had to wear skirts at parties. Third, you were not supposed to climb trees. Fourth, you got mesmerized. Fifth, he got educated. He did, you didn't. Oh, damn and damn the favouritism and beastliness of everybody and everybody and everybody.

But I will not sulk, she said to herself, and I will not let anybody see that I care, and instead of moping I will think in a brilliant manner about the entire situation, so that when Nicky comes back it will be plain to all that I am not merely a Plaything To Be Cast Aside, but a Person To Be Reckoned With, who has Made Discoveries, so there.

Oddly enough, and contrary to the usual experience of humans when feeling vengeful, she did make the discoveries, as planned.

"It is not because Nicky is a boy," she suddenly said out loud. It is because he can't be thought-read, while I can. That is why Dr. McTurk wanted him to spy on the Master, not me. Because with me, the Master would know I was spying and who for. I see. I see.

They kept us so as to blackmail Daddy and Uncle Pierrepoint, but when they found that Nicky was not mesmerizable they were pleased, because that kind of person is useful in whatever-it-is. And that's what he is being educated for. What for?

And Dr. McTurk, with all that gabble about atom-bombs and mental illnesses, and telling us not to tell anybody, wanted to use Nicky to get at the Master because the Master can't see what Nicky is thinking but he probably can see what the doctor is thinking, and the doctor is terrified of the Master which means that he must be plotting against him, so he has to do the plot through Nicky, who can't be seen through. Yes?

Yes.

The medicine.

He said something about medicine.

If Dr. McTurk wanted to poison the Master, he couldn't, because the old man would know what he was meaning to do.

Incidentally, no wonder he's terrified when he meets him. For fear of being read.

He has to keep away.

He might be read at any meeting, any moment. It's like having I AM GOING TO POISON YOU written on your forehead and having to go about with it in plain letters, chancing being seen.

Of course he is going to poison him. That's obvious. He will tell Nicky that the Master refuses to take the medicine which is good for him and he will ask Nicky to give it to him secretly and the Master won't know.

And the reason why he doesn't do it at once is because he doesn't know whether the Master has finished making whatever-it-is or not, and that is why he wants Nicky as an informer, and of course it is to get hold of whatever-it-is that he has to poison him!

In the ecstacy of this splendid piece of deduction,

Judy suddenly went flat. She thought: Poison? These things don't happen, not with fat little men like Santa Claus. I am being dramatic, I suppose.

But she thought also: Well, they did shoot at us.

And she concluded humbly: Anyway, Nicky may be interested in what I guessed.

He was interested, when he came back that evening from the examination, and very much so.

"Judy, you're a wizard! You've got it. It sticks out a mile. Do you remember how he said about 'a sedative for our honoured Master?' Of course he wants to kill him, it's just the greasy sort of thing he would do. And it's out of greed. He wants whatever-it-is."

"What is it?"

"Goodness knows."

"Could it be a Secret Weapon?"

"It could be anything, Judy. So far as I'm concerned, it might be a square on the hypotenuse!"

He told her about the joys of education.

"How can they possibly want you to know the date of Columbus?"

"Perhaps they just wanted a sort of I.Q."

"They didn't do anything about mesmerizing?"

"The Master wasn't even there."

"What was the Chinaman like?"

"He stood about."

"I wonder what he is."

"Well, for one thing he can talk without using words. We saw them. You know, about Jokey."

"Do you think he could be as old as the Master?"

"He might be."

"How old is the Master?"

"The antlers have the date they were killed underneath, on the plaque. It was 1879."

"They could have been killed by his father."

"Yes — or he could have been quite old when he killed them himself. It doesn't prove anything."

"He looks as if he was about a hundred."

"Or two hundred."

"But, Nicky, you can't be!"

"So far as that goes, you can't talk without words. Or mesmerize millions of workmen. Or hollow out an island in the middle of the Atlantic. Or practically anything they do."

He thought about it unhappily, and added a question.

"Is it *possible*, Judy, for us to outwit these kind of people?"

"Well," she said, after thinking it over, "it seems to me that children don't have so much experience as older people, but sometimes they are a good deal brighter. Look at poor old Totty for instance. All that stuff of his about Top Secrets wouldn't have fooled a cockroach."

CHAPTER ELEVEN

The Last of Totty

IF they could have looked at Totty, they would have looked away.

It was night, and the dark Atlantic, peaceful after fog, heaved mightily under the summer moon outside. The great rollers, whose unbroken crests were at least two hundred feet apart, seemed scarcely to rise or fall in the slithery moon track — but actually they rose from twenty to thirty feet. A seaplane might have thought it a flat calm and would have landed at its peril.

The mist had turned to rain before sunset. It had now cleared up, and the damp weather had livened a couple of Manx Shearwaters, which often come out at night. They flew fast, invisible in the darkness. Crossing the moon's carpet they became visible — skimming the swells so that they rose and fell with them as if floating on the sea though really in the air, now right wing up, now left, on rigid pinion mostly with few beats, clamouring as they sped. They cried "It's-*vour*-fault" and "It's-a-corker."

The black mass of Rockall stood in silhouette

against the velvet and the silver, like a wedge of cheese on its side. The stars were crisp in spite of the moonlight, everything washed too clear. Even the Razorbills and Guillemots who stood on the summit of the island could be seen as a kind of prickly fringe upon the outline, the latter standing upright like sentries on a vigil, the former laid on their chests, as if they were hatching.

The island had radar, to warn it of unwanted neighbours.

There were no neighbours now, so the casement of the Master's sitting-room was open — one of the three openings in the cliff face. Its mellow lamplight lay like golden syrup on the charmèd wave, challenging the lunar pathway, silent and lonely in the wilderness of waters — two hundred and fifty miles from anywhere.

If there had been a movie camera on hand, it would have tracked down to the window and gone in, to discover the ancient scientist in his Morris chair. The closer it came to the opening, the less the silence would have been. Music as well as lamplight was pouring into the night. The radiogram was at half volume. It was exhibiting, on a long-playing record, the fugal mathematics of Bach.

But the Master was not listening.

He sat in the old-fashioned chair as still as a cobra, his eyes fixed on the door. The soft paraffin-light gleamed on his cross-hatched skull of ivory.

The door opened as he watched it, and Dr. McTurk came in.

It was a horrible entry — a hair-raising one. For one

thing it was slow and silent. Rabbits which have been fascinated by stoats stay frozen and scream, but the Doctor's reluctance was soundless and in motion. He moved at a snail's pace, one foot before the other, each shoe extended like a bather testing water, sliding not lifting, stealthy and compelled. The door had opened as slowly as the footsteps. The man who was coming seemed like a creature who must move on tiptoe in the presence of some dreadful danger, not to be disturbed — a frog or toad, facing a green mamba, drawn forward and its bones dissolved to water by the unwinking eye.

He had been called.

He came to the Master in ghastly slow-motion, each one's eyes fixed upon the other's, and as he came to him the old man rose.

They faced each other without a syllable.

The sequence went into reverse — as a breaker reaching its furthest stretch draws out again — and now the Doctor, walking backwards, withdrew from the boudoir, followed by the skull. They walked as slowly as ever, pace by pace, eyes locked, keeping an exact distance. The Doctor, putting his hand behind him, found the door handle as if he could see. They turned left at the Axminster carpet and down the stairs they went, tread after tread, one foot going softly down as the other one's came forward.

In the narrow hall-way, the victim felt the wooden chest against the back of his knees. He lifted his hand above his head and grasped the antler — which he had never touched before.

The section of the wall swung open.

They moved into the laboratory, step for step, at funeral pace, treading their measure to the bloodless fugues of Bach.

The Doctor put one finger to a switch, which he had not known was there. He pressed, and the machine controlled by it began to whine. The blank tiled wall in front began to shimmer.

They came to rest.

Then — with a strangled shriek which would have turned your stomach to water — Dr. McTurk threw both his hands above his head and leaped — positively leaped — to face the thin high music of the vibrator unit.

CHAPTER TWELVE

Polonius

THEY missed him at once, but the odd thing was they did not mention it. Somehow, by not putting it into words, they could prevent the fact from coming real.

The brilliant stars which had shone the night he vanished had been the result of rain, not the foretaste of it. The weather settled down again to the dog days of the yacht's first coming.

Except for the afternoons — when Nicky had to go for his lessons — they spent the time on the grilled summit of the islet. They watched the busy Jokey having the worst of several arguments with a Fulmar. They talked about their parents; about the countryside of England in its full green so far away from them; about their ponies out at grass in the home park — about anything except the Doctor.

Nearly a week went by before they even got round to speaking of their own problem.

"When does the helicopter come back?"

"Mr. Frinton said he would be gone till Saturday."

"He doesn't seem to spend much time here."

"Perhaps he doesn't want to."

"I wish we could get away like him."

He stared towards the horizon, not answering, stretched at full length and propped on his elbows. The sea below them was improbably blue, like an advertisement for Florida. A Puffin was whirring on its bee-line to somewhere or other, quite close, so that they could see the crimson ring round its eye and the steely triangle above it. What funny birds Puffins are, he thought, like solemn clowns! It must be the eye-triangles, which clowns have. And that's why people give them nicknames, like "Bottlenose" or "Tommy Noddie". It's more the eyemarks than the rainbow beak.

"Judy, do you see? His hands are folded!"

"What?"

"The Puffin's. Look! Quick!"

"So they are!"

"Under his tail coat. Like an alderman."

"Well I never!"

He cast about in his memory and added, "I read in a book somewhere that one of their nicknames is the Pope."

"He must be praying as he flies. Were the palms together?"

"What a nice tubby Pope he is — with a bottlenose and circus make-up!"

"And he waddles on the land."

"More like a nautical roll."

"Nicky, people may be bad at *Bello Gallico*, but it's nice not to be dumb with birds. It is nice to know about birds."

When the Puffin banked, it unfolded the red hands

98

and spread them wide on each side of its tail, using them like the elevators of an aeroplane.

"It said in the book," he explained, accepting her compliment, "that Puffins fly 'with unctuous palms'. What is unctuous?"

They left it at that.

"Ju?"

"Yes?"

"The only way to escape would be on the trawler or in the helicopter."

"Could we ask Mr. Frinton to take us?"

"Ape!"

"He doesn't seem so bad as . . . as some were."

"Obviously you can't ask him when he's working for the Master! What do you think?"

"There isn't room to stow away in it, not without being found."

"So far as that goes it would be a frightful job stowing away in the trawler, specially with Jokey."

"We couldn't leave Jokey."

"Of course not."

"Nicky?"

"Well?"

"These foul nightgowns. Can't we get some proper clothes somehow, to cut down or something? I'm getting sick of looking like cherubim. Would Mr. Frinton order some in Ireland? We could give him our measurements to take."

"I wonder," he reflected, "if we could hide a note

in the helicopter. Not about clothes, but about
rescuing us. There must be somebody at the other
end who services it, and he might find a message if we
hid it in the engine somewhere. . . ."

"Let's send a message in a bottle."

He turned his head sideways on the brown elbow
and looked at her with one reproachful eye. So do
admirals examine sub-lieutenants, and in a similar
silence.

"Well, they *might* find it."

Silence.

"Mightn't they?"

He stopped looking. Her ignorance was too
odious for comment.

"Porpoises!" she exclaimed.

He shot upright at once. Porpoises were their
favourite fish, or rather mammal.

"Where?"

They were nearly half a mile away, but coming
towards the island. The great, gleaming backs rose
one after the other, perhaps in chase of fish upon the
surface, perhaps in pure delight and blithesomely. The
lubricated, streamlined, glistening shoulders split the
sea in turns as they came nearer — or sometimes was it
the same one? They sliced or slid or slipped between
the elements of air and water, making a slow and
curving roll or rocking-horse or see-saw, head up, then
tail. But neither head nor tail quite surfaced. A school
of porpoises! If they had been a school of children
bathing, they might have dived from sky to sea. The
ocean scholars dived from sea to sky. It was exciting

to wait for each appearance, to count them as they came and pray they would come nearer.

"They are not hunting," said Nicky. "If they were after a shoal of fish, the Gannets would be there too. They are doing it for fun."

They did come nearer. The line-ahead of arching submarines drew closer and closer at each rise, till you could have dropped a biscuit on the nearest back. The back came out directly under them, its friendly eye emerging from the water-level with a kind of jocularity, fixing the twins with a hint of a wink and sinking with the self-satisfied smirk of keen intelligence, like a devil on the trap-door at a pantomime. The eye of humour was the fulcrum of the see-saw.

"How lovely it would be to pat them," said Judy.

"You know," he said in a muffled voice, looking down at the hot rock between his arms, one inch from his nose, "if we did escape, it would be kind of running away."

"We could fetch help."

"Yes."

"We can't do anything here. Not just us, by ourselves."

"If we could escape, we ought to, I suppose. People ought to be told."

"They could send the Navy."

"Would people believe us much, do you think?"

"I don't see why not."

"We should have to take some sort of proof. Steal one of Pinky's scanners or something."

"The difficulty would be getting on the trawler without being seen."

"Could we put Jokey in a suitcase?"

"If we had a suitcase."

"I won't go without Jokey."

"Nobody asked you."

"And she's bound to bark," she added unhappily.

After a pause, he went back to the original theme.

"It *would* be running away, Ju. It's uncomfortable."

"He who fights and . . ."

"I know all that. But what can we *tell* them? It's no good telling them what's going on here if we don't know."

"We could tell them about . . . about the Doctor."

"I suppose it's true."

"Yes."

"He can't be locked up somewhere, can he?"

"Where?"

"We haven't seen . . . a body."

"Look at those gulls."

A neat Kittiwake who had caught a fish was being harried round the sky by a Skua. It's mouth was too full to say anything, but the Skua was yelling like a hellion — *skeer, skeerr* — as the stern chase jinked and dodged about the aether, in a flap of buffeting wings, feinting talons and cries of terrifying ferocity. The Kittiwake swallowed the fish and screamed, *kit, kit*, in fear or indignation, but the pursuit was relentless. It sicked up the fish, which fell, a dark object drawing away from the other two in the air. And instantly the

Skua had swept into a dive on a half roll, stooping like a Falcon in a power-assisted descent, flying down, not falling, and there it was with the booty in its shearing beak — shaped like secateurs — before the fish had touched the water. The pirate made off with every sign of satisfaction, while the Kittiwake sailed sulkily home, remarking, "Unfair to legitimate competition."

"Liquidated," said Nicky heavily, not thinking of Skuas or Kittiwakes.

The resilience of the children, which was largely ignorance and optimism, did have moments of starkness when they glimpsed their position.

"Nick . . ."

She was going to say she was afraid, but she didn't. The fact was, she was afraid to say so.

". . . How are you getting on with being educated?"

"It's dopey."

"What do you do?"

"Nothing."

"Nothing?"

"Well, it's not like learning anything. You just read books.

"As a matter of fact," he added with shame, "I like them."

"What sort of books?"

"H. G. Wells and Julian Huxley and that sort of thing, with pictures of prehistoric animals and diagrams of the Descent of Man — like a Mexican cactus. G. Elliott Smith. Dr. Lorenz. They have a set of Witherby. And there's the one about how Black-headed Gulls will sit on tobacco tins instead of eggs."

"I don't see what bird books have got to do with being a gangster."

"It's about the Animal Kingdom."

"Are they kind to you?"

"I don't know.

"You see," he explained, "they mostly leave me alone. The Chinaman brings books from somewhere, and the old man has only looked at me twice."

He considered the matter attentively and added, "It's like being a dog."

"How do you mean?"

"If you talk to Jokey, you have to say 'Sit' or 'Basket' or 'Walkies'. It's no good saying, 'To be or not to be, that is the question'."

She was still puzzled.

He said with effort, thinking it out and searching for words, "Listen. I think he has forgotten how to talk. When he talks to the Chinaman it is in some kind of language which is beyond us, like quoting Shakespeare would be beyond Jokey. So when he has to say something for me to understand, it is an effort for him. It is difficult for him to press it together — all his meaning — like putting 'Shall we go out together for a country stroll' into 'walkies'. And that's why, when he does say something, it's generally a motto or a proverb or something, which has a lot of meaning in it already. Do you see?"

"What has he said?"

"Nothing actually. But he did write two things down."

Nicky rolled over on his back and produced two

crumpled slips of paper from the nightshirt pocket, about quarter the size of a postcard. On these there was written in an exquisite rather Greek handwriting, "*Ham*. III. iv. 29." and "Nescis, mi fili, quantillâ prudentiâ mundus regatur." The accents were marked with careful courtesy.

"Why will he talk Latin?" asked Judy pettishly.

"I don't think he does it on purpose. If the nearest quotation is in Latin, he uses it, but if it was in Arabic or double Dutch or whatever else he used to talk, he would use that too. As a matter of fact, I think he'd rather have English, like when he said Waste-Not-Want-Not, but sometimes there isn't an English one that's suitable."

"What does it mean?"

"There was a Latin dictionary for my General Knowledge Paper, so I worked it out. It means more or less 'Little dost thou know, my son, with what a small stock of wisdom the world is governed'."

"And what does *that* mean?"

"I don't know. I was reading about how stupid the gulls who sit on tobacco tins are and he came in and stood opposite me and just looked. Judy, when they are silent it isn't an act, you see, they just are. He was sort of trying to see what I was thinking, like we try to see what Jokey is, and then he tried to give me a message like saying 'Seek' to Jokey. He looked at the gull book and he looked at me and then he wrote it down. Do you think he meant that men are like gulls?"

Judy was not interested in proverbs.

"What about the other one?"

"It was the day after the Doctor . . . you know." He took a breath and added, "As a matter of fact, I asked him."

"Nick!"

"Well, he came in while I was reading and sort of examined me like a postage stamp or something, like when you use a magnifying glass on it and . . . oh, yes, by the way, he drank a lot of whisky both times, before he wrote anything at all . . . And . . . Well, I suddenly just said, 'What did you do to the Doctor?' "

"Oh, Nicky, you are brave!"

"He took out his pen and wrote."

She read the slip with care.

"I believe he wrote it down like the Latin because he knew I would have to work it out. If it was easy, like 'Waste-Not-Want-Not', he would have said it, wouldn't he, but it was written so that I could look it up?"

"Do you know what it is?" she asked triumphantly.

"No?"

"It's a quotation from Shakespeare."

"Ju!"

"*Hamlet*."

"There's a Shakespeare in the ship's library. Let's go and see."

They went helter-skelter to the hangar doors and to the lift, leaving sunlight for the artificial day. Behind them on the noonday summit, the retractable radar aerial, which could be drawn back into the rock, turned ceaselessly through its silent angle of 360°, sweeping the empty sky.

Polonius

Riffling through the grubby pages of a much-used copy, they found the lines at once.

These said:

Thou wretched, rash, intruding fool, farewell! I took thee for thy better.

CHAPTER THIRTEEN

A Present from China

WHEN the children separated for the boy's afternoon lesson, they were both thinking about escape. It
was not that they sat down to consider it in a logical
way, but their minds scurried about like mice in a large
cage, picking up a crumb here and there, nibbling it,
swallowing it or spitting it out and then scampering
elsewhere.

Nicky sat alone in the boudoir, not attending to the
wonderful illustrations of Forel's book about ants
which was on his knees.

The objections to stowing away on the trawler were
practical ones. It might be fairly easy to stow away
among the comings and goings of a large liner in a
busy port, but it was not possible in the circumstances
of Rockall. There were only eleven people left on the
island, which meant that it would be quick and easy
to be missed from among them. Nor had they been
allowed on board the ship. This meant that they would
be spotted at once if they tried to slip aboard — and
how, incidentally, were they to do it, since there was
no pier or gangway? They could hardly cadge a lift

in the ship's boat or from the crane, carrying the dog with them. It also meant that they would not know where to hide. They had no picture in their minds of the inside of her, and would be stumbling along iron ladders and passages looking for they knew not what refuge, at the risk of meeting one of the seamen at any turn.

Does one, he wondered, stick oneself down in the coal bunkers (under coal) or, worse still, under the fish? Are the fish kept loose, like coal, or perhaps salted and put in refrigerators or something, and do trawlers have "ship's life-boats", under the lashings of which he knew it was usual to conceal stowaways?

No. He was a common-sense boy and he saw that however easy it was to hide on strange ships in adventure stories, it would be difficult in life. His sister and he were country children from Somerset, not sailors, and for that matter they did not even know whether the trawler was coal-burning or diesel. For them a sheet was something to put on a bed — not, as mariners mysteriously have it, a piece of rope — and he was sensible enough to see that they would be asking for trouble if they tried to play monkey-tricks with a different sort of world from their own.

The helicopter was even more out of the question. You might as well try to hide in a shop window. The only way to get away in it, would have been to fly it.

Perhaps, on the whole, people are inclined to do what they are doing rather than make the effort of trying something else. They prefer the frying pan to the fire. They give in to the Moment of Inertia. Anyway, Nicky dismissed the two escape routes from his mind without enough of a struggle.

He had forgotten about hiding a note in the helicopter — which would have been a first rate thing to try — because his sister's question about bottles had driven it out of his head.

He thought, Well, we shall have to see what happens. This may have been weak of him, but it was wise. (If you are either of these things you generally have to be the other.) On the other hand, it is nice to think that both of them were willing to sacrifice their liberty rather than betray Jokey.

His mind flitted to a different side of the muddle.

Squadron-Leader Frinton was seldom on the island. He seemed to deliver stores or whatever it was, like a messenger boy, and then be off again as soon as possible. Except for his black beard and obvious expression of piracy — if not cruelty — he seemed almost as if he might be dodging the Master as the wretched Totty had done. Nor was the negro any use as a clue. There remained the two main figures.

It is all very well snooping round, thought Nicky, and asking one person questions about another. The thing we haven't tried is asking people about themselves. Why can't we demand to be told?

The idea of demanding anything from the Master exploded of its own accord. It was impossible, like breathing under water.

There was left the Chinaman.

Suppose — he supposed — I tried to screen him? At

least they can't punish you for asking questions. And there are lots of questions about the Chinaman which might help to solve our riddles. How do you begin?

When the impassive figure came to collect the volume of Forel at tea time, Nicky still did not know where to start. So he took a deep breath and set off bravely in the middle.

"How old are you?"

"Fifty-eight."

"How old is the Master?"

"That you must ask him."

"What are you making?"

"That also."

"Can we go home soon?"

"No."

"Why not?"

A labour-saving way of answering the question would have been to use the well-worn nursery answer, "Because not." The Chinaman was more economical — he made no reply at all.

It was a full answer, because it left the boy to work it out for himself.

"Will we ever get loose?"

"Yes."

"When?"

Silence.

It was not a rude silence, it was a No Bid one — like a card player passing a call or somebody having an argument who decides not to make a comment which would only lead to further explanations.

At about this stage in the talk, the beginning of it

began to catch up with Nicky. I wish, he thought, I hadn't begun by asking his age like that. He will think that I was rude to him because he was Chinese, although the real reason was that I was too scared to think of anything else. Ought I to say I'm sorry? No, that would make it worse. You can't explain.

Not knowing how to put the next question, he said it like this, "Are you fond of the Master?"

"No."

The reply baffled him. He had to start again.

"Do you mind me asking questions? I am not trying to be rude."

"You have both been patient and polite."

The calm face suddenly summoned a smile of real kindness and added with a twinkle, "I must apologize for shooting at you."

"Not at all."

He felt that this was silly. He covered it up by asking quickly, "If you are not fond of the Master, why do you work for him?"

"I am not fond of anybody."

"Are you mesmerized like the others?"

"No."

"*Are* they mesmerized?"

The Chinaman felt in one of the long sleeves which could be used to hold pistols and produced three delicate bowls, about the size of egg cups but more graceful, and a small jug or pitcher to match them. They were of Satsuma china. The jug had water in it already. He handed the bowls to Nicky so that he could examine them.

A Present from China

The thin porcelain had a round glass blob or lens or optic at the bottom of each bowl, made of plain glass.

The Chinaman tilted the jug to fill them with water and, as the water came out, it sang like a Nightingale. It really did make musical trills with the liquid notes of that bird, quite loud. Then he pointed to the bowls. Inside the optic of each one there had appeared an old-fashioned photograph of a geisha-girl, rather in the style of a daguerrotype, and the girls were peeping at him coyly from behind their fans.

Nicky was flabbergasted.

"What did you do?"

"Do it yourself."

He emptied the bowls into the pampas vase and handed them over. The jug still had water in it, and it still sang, even for Nicky, and the girls — who had vanished when the bowls were empty — came back.

"!"

"It is a present for your sister."

By the time he had done it twice more, and used up the water, the Chinaman had faded away.

Meanwhile, Judy had been working on the problem also. It was all very well for Nicky to sneer at her scheme about a bottle, but what she wanted to know was, why not? It *might* be found and it did not cost anything to send. If there was a possibility, why not try it? Nicky might or might not know whether Rockall was in the Gulf Stream, and where the Gulf Stream went, but the fact that there was no charge for bottles had a strong influence on Judy, who was a housewifely sort of person. Besides, she was feeling obstinate. Men might spend their time educating one another, and leaving women to less important jobs if any, but she was a bit of a suffragette. She was not going to be ignored and snubbed. Why *shouldn't* a bottle be found? Also, while her brother was away, she had nothing else to do. How pleasant it would be — what a terrific suck-in — if by her own efforts, alone and scorned, a message could be sent to the mainland!

She cadged a bottle from Pinky in the kitchen and stole some paper from a prescription-pad in the empty surgery, where there was also a ball pen.

She wrote:

> Please send this message to Major-General the Duke of Lancaster, M.F.H., the Stables, Gaunt's Godstone, Somerset and please Mrs. Henderson to deliver it with the milk please.

If she told them that an international plot had kidnapped them into the hollowed-out inside of a solid island, would the letter be believed, or would it be taken as a hoax? On the other hand, it was no good just saying that they were there, because the yacht would obviously have searched. She decided to compromise, and went on:

> Please come and fetch us off as we are still on Rockall as we were swept inside and you will see a square kind of window at water level and this is my hair to prove it, Ju.

She managed with difficulty to break off not very

much hair — no scissors — then remembered the hospital ones, and cut off a proper lock. She unfolded the letter to add "Love to all", corked the bottle as tightly as she could and made her way to the ledge outside the hangar doors. The bottle dived in with a distant plop and shot out again because of the air inside. Then it began sauntering about at the foot of the cliff, dilly-dallying, not making any effort to go to England.

Judy and Jokey looked round them in the sunlight. The vast horizons were empty. The radar aerial moved steadily and secretly, like the brains of some prehistoric monster. The cups of the anemometer chased each other in an endless circle, and the arm which showed the wind direction for the helicopter pointed south-west.

When Nicky brought her the Chinaman's gift of magic, she was enchanted.

"It's not so much the present," she said primly, "it's the *thought*."

But the present itself was exquisite. They spent the whole evening messing about with water, and Jokey was in raptures about the Nightingale. She stood with her head on one side, and what appeared to be one ear in what appeared to be one eye, waiting for the bird to come out and licking her lips. Sometimes she gave a yap to encourage it and sometimes a sort of nip at the bottle, like a boxer pretending to hit you but missing you on purpose.

Nicky said, "It is something to do with (what is it called?) like when a stick looks bent in water. When the bowls are empty, you can't see the girls because the bent rays prevent it, but the water corrects the glass somehow, and then you can see them. But *how* does the jug sing?"

It had a narrow neck, which prevented them from seeing inside. They never did find out.

CHAPTER FOURTEEN

The Diaries

"Nicky."

"?"

"Where do your books come from?"

"How do you mean?"

"There is only one shelf in the boudoir."

"I suppose there must be a library somewhere."

"We ought to explore the Private Side."

"Why?"

"Well, there must be other rooms. For one thing, where do they sleep? The Chinaman lives there with him, so there must be two bedrooms at least. Probably whatever they are making is in there too."

"I can't explore when I'm sent for. They dump me in a chair by the radiogram and keep coming in and out."

"Could we get in at night, do you suppose, while they're alseep?"

"You are very adventurous suddenly."

"I wonder if they have a bathroom?" reflected Judy. Her interest was domestic. She wondered whether it would be proper plumbing or a geyser.

Nicky's interest of the moment was also homely.

"Judy, if we got our overalls back, why couldn't you sew them up the seams?"

"I could!"

"Well, then."

"And we can stop squeaking and gibbering in the streets of Rome!"

"?"

"It's a quotation from Julius Caesar, and these are our togas."

She held out the skirts of the now despised night-shirt and began to pirouette round the empty hangar with ghoulish motions, in imitation of the Roman spectres mentioned by the bard.

"If we did get in at night," said Nicky, "we could read his diaries."

It was her turn to make a question mark.

"The shelf in the boudoir is all diaries."

"How do you know?"

"They have dates printed on the back in gold."

"They could be calendars or something."

"Yes."

"What dates?"

"The first one is 1849."

"How could he have written a diary in 1849?"

She counted on her fingers, one finger for each ten till she got to 1949, after which she would have to use her toes in secret, for the digits. Unfortunately, on reaching ten fingers, she remembered that the year nought was in the first century, which confused the issue.

"I suppose they could be Tide Tables or something,"

said Nicky, "but even then I don't know why he wants tide tables for 1849. Perhaps they are astronomy."

"People use soap for making keys."

"Try thinking about something, darling."

"Yes, they do. They steal the key and press it on a bit of soap and then they have the impression of the key and . . ."

"I know all that, you oaf, but you can't make the *key* out of soap. All you have got is the impression."

"We could ask Pinky to make one."

He stopped.

"I wonder if it would be safe?"

"If they have cut out his tongue to stop him talking to us, it stops him talking to them."

"Do you think they really have?"

"Perhaps he didn't have one to begin with."

She added, "Nicky, *can* all this be happening? I mean, if the Chinaman is kind and gives us lovely presents *how* could they cut out Pinky's tongue?"

"It wasn't lately, anyway."

"Any time would be horrible."

"And why not everybody else's?"

"Perhaps he bit it off," said Judy hopefully, "in an accident."

"Anyway I don't see how I could steal the key, to begin with."

"Is there one?"

"I don't know."

"Next time you go, look inside the door."

"The door opens of its own accord, don't you remember?"

"Oh, dear!"

"There will be some foul invisible ray or something."

"Or you can stand on mats."

"There isn't a mat."

"It could be under the felt carpet, like when Mummy rings for the next course at dinner."

"I suppose it could."

"Nicky, I don't want to go."

"Well, it was you who said to go."

"Doors opening by themselves and everything."

He said, "*If* I get a chance, I mean if I'm certain they are both busy, I might be able to get a peep at the diaries."

He did, and they were diaries, as he had suspected.

The first one began in a slanting hand with dashes instead of full stops. It said, "March 24th, 1849 — The way to live for ever is to find some reason for doing so — "

At that moment, the Chinaman came in.

The boy's heart jumped into his gullet and stuck there for a moment, choking him, then turned over and dived. It lodged above his knees. He shoved the book back among the others.

There was no comment.

CHAPTER FIFTEEN

A Glimpse of Everest

On Saturday nights, there was a change in the feeling of the island. When it was fine weather they sometimes sat on the peak till bed-time, watching the stars pricked out of their expanding universe and the dizzy sweep of the Milky Way, which makes you feel as if you were arching over backwards yourself. What a sight that vapour was — the silvery wood-smoke in the void of space! They were country-bred children. Although they were not clever at irregular verbs, they could tell birds by their songs and trees by their look and the usual animals by instinct. For instance, they never looked at the colours of a bird when you asked them what it was. They simply said its name at once, and could not explain why they knew. If pressed, they would say in a worried tone, Well, it flies like that — or, Well, it just is.

They were fairly well up in stars too. They had a landsman's knowledge of their favourite ones — not a sailor's. They knew Orion because he was a hunter, and Sirius particularly, because he was a dog, and of course they knew Cassiopeia, because you can find the

North Star by cutting her widest angle in two. Arc-
turus was real for them when it could be seen, because
they had been told it had the same name as King
Arthur in Sir Thomas Malory, and there were various
other more or less random ones which had caught their
fancy. Nicky had different choices from Judy. One of
the splendid things about the constellations was that
there were none named after cats.

On most nights, as they sat among the roosting
birds who accepted them without protest, there was
music from beneath them. The three casements of
Rockall were cut in the vertical side, one under the
other. When there were no aircraft or ships in the
offing, the middle window opened after dinner in the
evening and, with the lamplight, came the counter-
point of radiogram — sometimes Haydn or Palestrina,
but nearly always Bach. It was played at half strength.

On Saturdays a change came over the programme,
which altered from mathematics to emotion.

As they sat there spell-bound, far into the night, the
powerful machine at its fullest volume absolutely
hurled its thunder into the dark, so that the granite
eyrie seemed to rock and sway beneath their feet, like
a belfry. Sometimes there were real bells. The rumpus
at the end of the *Overture 1812*, with all the peals and
pigeons and cannons and national anthems going off in
all directions — for surely a very small and distant
Czar in a white uniform is standing at the top of a great
range of steps then, while flights of doves, snowflakes,
confetti and anything else you like go whirling with
the bells and glory of victory — this would come

early in the evening, probably followed by the first pianoforte concerto by the same composer. As the night grew wilder, there would be Boleros and Danses Macabres, bits of Rachmaninoff and Mussorgsky and Dohnanyi, until at last the orgy came to an end with Rimsky-Korsakov and *Prince Igor* — the deafening riot of the Polovtsian dances in Act 2. It was tremendous.

The Master hardly ever played Beethoven, Handel or Mozart, except fugues. He was not a Prince of Light like these three.

The twins were sitting in the starshine on the Saturday evening after the helicopter got back, feeling as if they ought to hold on to prevent themselves being blasted off by Ravel, who was going on below. They could hardly talk without shouting.

"I wish we could see what he's doing."

"He sounds drunk."

"Do you think he *can* be drunk?"

"Look at the whisky he has before he says anything."

"It doesn't seem to make much difference."

"It makes the difference that he speaks."

"If Daddy had all that, he would want to sing the Boating Song — or do the trick with asparagus."

"Or fall down."

"Nicky!"

"Well, anyway, he would suddenly look vague and march off to bed without saying anything. Three full tumblers must be nearly a bottle."

"Do you think he is . . . like that?"

"He might get drunk on Saturday nights on purpose, for some reason, like bath nights."

"Why?"

"Judy, how can I know? But he does do things for reasons. He's not mad."

This struck her for the first time.

"Are you sure he isn't?"

"Quite sure."

"If he is drunk, we might be able to get in and search the other rooms or read the diaries."

"Or be shot. How do you know he isn't sitting there with the Chinaman's pistol, shooting V.R. on the ceiling like Sherlock Holmes?"

"Anyhow," she said doubtfully, "there's the black door and we haven't got a key."

"I tell you it doesn't have a key."

"Just listen to that!"

It was the Scherzo of Brahms' *Quintet in F minor*, arranged for two pianos.

Nicky said, pondering, "The three windows are one above the other. If we had a rope we could climb down from the hangar door and look in. At least we could see what he's doing."

"Could we let ourselves down on the crane?"

"It would make too much row. Anyway I don't know how to work it."

"Couldn't you find out, Nicky?"

"Not silently, I don't think."

"Is there a rope?"

"There's bound to be ropes in the store-room, but it's locked."

"Could we tie some sheets together? They do in escape stories."

"They say they do."

"Why not?"

"Well, look, Judy, a sheet is about ten feet long and when you've tied a big knot at both ends, how much do you think you have left? You'd need about two sheets to go the length of a man."

"Anyway, it would be frightfully dangerous."

"Yes."

"Suppose he looked out!"

Ta-Ra-Ra-Ra, Tiddledee-Tum-tum-tum, went the scherzo, Tiddledee tum, tiddledee tum, tiddledee tum.

"But when the Chinaman caught me, he didn't do a thing."

"I believe he's nice."

"He certainly missed us with the pistol," said her brother sarcastically.

Be not afeared, poor Caliban once explained in *The Tempest*, the isle is full of noises, sounds and sweet airs that give delight and hurt not. Even the inside of the island, as they sank in the lift on their way to bed, was thrumming with the triumph of the pianos. It came up the shaft.

"Could we possibly hear through the black door?"

They looked at one another, guessing, and simultaneously their hands went to the button which would take them to the private landing.

At the end of the gleaming corridor the ebony door stood open.

It looked far away.

There was no means of going back, once they had launched themselves on the passage — no side turnings or nooks in the straight, white tunnel, into which they could dodge and hide. Once they started, they must go on.

It made them whisper.

"Suppose he isn't drunk, Nicky?"

"Why should he be?"

"We only thought he might be."

"I didn't."

"Would he do what he did to the doctor?"

Tum tum tumty tum!

"Ju, you stay here. I believe I could go along and if I'm caught I could pretend I had left a book behind or something."

"Don't you dare leave me alone."

"But I'm more or less allowed to go there and you're not."

"I won't stay alone."

"Judy. . . ."

She tossed her head and began to march down the corridor, which at least forced him not to desert her.

"Judy. . . ."

He had to run to catch up.

"You might at least wait a minute. We've got to think."

She waited.

"What are we trying to do?"

"Explore the rooms and read the diaries."

"But we can't possibly read the diaries if he is play-

ing the radiogram right beside them. Besides, why do
we want to read them?"

"They will say what he is inventing," she said.

"Even then. Right beside him!"

"He may be asleep."

"In that racket?"

For some reason she had become as brave as a
lion — no, a lioness.

"It doesn't matter. He won't do anything. We
are children."

"But. . . ."

"You're afraid."

The record changed itself with a sigh, rumbled for a
moment and was off with a great crash into the
dramatics of some Russian or other, probably hammer-
ing on a coffin lid. He was not playing the discs in
any particular order.

"I'm not."

"Then come on."

"Judy, don't be mad. If we go, we must go softly.
We *must not* be caught."

"Cowboys and Indians then."

"Yes."

"Like the elopement in *H.M.S. Pinafore*," said
Judy, whose musical tastes were more on that level.
Their father was a great man for Gilbert and Sullivan.

"I wish you wouldn't be so reckless. This is
serious."

"Silent be! It was the cat!"

"Judy!"

"Oh, all right."

And suddenly she was again as scared as he was.

They tip-toed down the long stretch of felt, feeling at every moment that they were further and further from their lines of communication. Indeed, even half way along, they knew that they had crossed the Rubicon.

"Don't tread near the door," breathed Nicky, "in case there's a bell or something. Go round the edges."

"Don't whisper."

"Why not?"

"Don't talk at all."

They could have shouted without making much odds, but the deference of fear made them silent. At the same time, there was a thrill about stealth — an elation like fizzy lemonade. It was wonderful to be young, alive, mobile, agile, secret, able, in danger.

The hall looked the same as ever, the visiting cards undisturbed.

I wonder who dusts, thought Judy — her mind working on two different levels, as it sometimes did in a crisis.

At the top of the stairs, the painted door was half open, ruling a wedge of light across the Axminster.

They went up on hands and knees, moving as slowly as chameleons do on their leafy sticks at the Zoo. Nicky was in the lead and had decided not to look round the door at the usual level. At carpet level, his movement might be less likely to catch the attention of a listener inside.

He held his head close to the floor and dipped it into the lamplight not faster than the minute hand of a clock, like this: first one ear, then the cheek bone, then one eye. One was enough. He reached back with his left hand and pressed Judy's, willing her to be still.

People talk of cutting a stuffy atmosphere with a knife. You could have divided the solid noise of the Master's room into biscuits with a pastry cutter. It poured out of the bright opening — in a wall, a tidal-wave, a bore. It engulfed them and battered them like a burst dam, the whole room reeling and shuddering as it was swept away by a new disc — the Polovtsian dances. In the middle of the stunning uproar, like a rock in a torrent, the Master sat with his eyes closed, his chin on his chest. He was wearing a quilted smoking-jacket and a round cap like a pill-box with a tassel — eerie, like a skeleton in rouge and lipstick. Three bottles of whisky stood beside him on the radiogram, the glass beside them chiming at the deep notes. His crackled face was infinitely distant in time and knowledge, blindly presiding over tumult in a world of stillness and silence, like a glimpse of Everest.

Something made Nicky turn his head.

Two steps below them, on the thick stair carpet, the Squadron-Leader was standing with an old-fashioned service revolver, his face contorted with fury.

CHAPTER SIXTEEN

The Squadron-Leader

Mr. Frinton put the weapon in the pocket of his duffle coat, took the twins by the scruff of their night-shirts — one strong hand for each — and hoisted them to their feet. Without saying a word, all three began walking backwards down the staircase, feeling for the steps.

At the foot of the stairs, he paused.

Then he turned them round, still powerless in his grip, and marched them out of the hall, along the passage, into the lift. It went up. He clanged the gate, walked them along the familiar corridor, kicked open his own door and pushed them inside.

He sat down on the bed, put his head in his hands as if he were going to cry, and said, "Damn!"

When he looked up again, the rage in his face had melted into the touching smile which they had seen before.

"Pay no regard."

"Is something the matter?" asked Judy kindly. She had not got so far as seeing the Master round the door, like Nicky, and, although bewildered, she noticed at once that Mr. Frinton needed comfort. Nicky was too breathless to say or think anything.

"You might say so."

"What is it?"

"Never mind."

"We have to mind, you see," she explained. "We have been kidnapped."

"I know."

"You might tell us."

"Oh God!" said Mr. Frinton, with a sort of exasperation. "You have only messed up a first class murder."

"Who was going to be murdered?"

"The Master, of course."

"We wouldn't mind."

He said heavily, "Yes, but would he?"

Then he stood up with a jerk and added, "You had better go to bed. Don't go near that place again. Just don't, you see? You are upsetting things."

Nicky asked, "Were you going to shoot him?"

"Yes."

"Could you have?"

"That is what we want to know."

"But I thought you were . . ."

"Listen, honeys, will you please go to bed?"

"No."

He suddenly seemed to realize that they were attractive, and they realized that he was. He laughed and said, "Honestly, there is no future in this for kids." Once you got over the black beard, and stopped looking at it, the other parts of his face were full of kindness and intelligence.

Judy said, "*Please* tell us what is going on. It's all very well being grown-up about it, but you don't know how nerve-racking it is for us, being pushed about without knowing what's happening or why. It's *much* worse, being shielded."

"Very well. I was going to have a crack at the old bod. But I can't do it with you two on the doorstep. . . ."

He paused.

"Well . . ."

Then, in desperation, "Oh, go to bed! It's impossible to know what goes on. I can't press on with this, with half the kindergarten underfoot."

"We are sorry."

"Pay no regard."

For them — who had been born in the thermonuclear age into a childhood which only thought about flying saucers and interplanetary weapons — his air force slang was out of date. The "prangs" and "pieces of cake" which had once been the common idiom of courage were old men's weaknesses for them. It made them feel awkward and protective when he used the language of bygone battles.

He sensed this and said abruptly, "Look, you must go to your room. I am busy."

"Why?"

"Just go."

They had reached the door when he sat down again, put his head in his hands for the second time and said in a voice of despair, "But I can't, with children on the island! I ought to get you out before I try."

They waited in silence.

"Your names are Nicky and Judy, aren't they?"

"Yes."

"I must think of a way of shipping you off."

"Could you take us in the helicopter?"

"No."

"Why not?"

"Because he would put the influence on us."

"Do you mean mesmerism?"

"No. The vibrator units."

"I'm afraid we don't know what vibrator units are."

"You are in good company."

Judy sat on the bed beside him and said, "If you want us to go back to our room so that you can go and shoot the Master, I don't think you ought to. It might be dangerous."

"That's what I thought."

"He might kill you instead."

"It's an idea, Judy."

"And then where would we be?"

"Just."

"So it would be wiser to explain things."

He seemed displeased by this, saying, "What is the good of talking?"

"We are not absolutely dumb," Nicky said.

Mr. Frinton gave another of his ravishing smiles, splitting the blue-black whiskers with square, white, even teeth, and apologized.

"I am being selfish. What do you want to know?"

What did they?

133

The boy produced the first question in his head, at random.

"How old is the Master?"

"He will be 157 on March 24th. He started his diaries on his fiftieth birthday and I have read them — that is, the parts you can read."

"How old?"

"One hundred and fifty-seven."

They made no comment — no protest or question.

"Dr. Moreau," Mr. Frinton went on, "was experimenting on his island and the *Iron Pirate* was at sea and *She* was living her immortal life in Africa when the Master was about ninety. Stevenson wrote *Treasure Island* when he was eighty-four. Captain Nemo was sailing in the *Nautilus* when he was seventy. Henry Russell Wallace thought of the origin of species when he was around sixty. Mary Shelley wrote *Frankenstein* when he was coming of age, and at the battle of Waterloo he was four years older than you are."

"When was the French Revolution?" asked Judy blankly.

"I can't remember."

"Why?"

"Why what?"

"How can he live so long as that?"

"It's all yours."

"But if . . ."

Nicky asked, "Is it a medicine?"

"I don't think so."

"Will he live for ever?"

"No."

"How do you know?"

"Because he is looking for successors. You are one of them."

"Me?"

"So am I."

Judy asked, "Has Nicky got to live for ever?"

"Not at this rate."

He cheered up, saying, "Look, I can't do anything now. I will have to think. Let me make us a cup of cocoa and I'll tell you what I can. We are talking in riddles."

While he was pottering with the chocolate powder, Judy asked, "Is this true? Dr. McTurk gave us a lot of stuff about Top Secrets, but it was lies. You are not telling lies?"

"It is too true, Judy, I'm afraid — as Totty would have said himself, when he went Austrylian."

"Was his name really McTurk?"

"No. He was a ship's surgeon called Jones. I believe he was a Welshman. I thought he was a bit of a diddler."

"Is he dead?"

The airman looked away.

"How?"

"Just dead."

"Was it the vibrator unit?"

After a struggle about whether to answer or not, for he did not want to chat about Totty's exit with children, he nodded.

"Why?"

"You could say he was planning a double-cross."

"He wanted to be the Master?"

"I suppose so."

"They call it," said Judy, producing one of her unsuspected bits of information, "a *coup d'état.*"

Nicky's mind bounced off hers into another digression.

"Do you think," he asked, "we could have our jeans back?"

"I'll try to get them tomorrow. Here's your cocoa."

They sat, burning their tongues on the hot stuff so that they could not taste it far back, as chocolate ought to be tasted. They moved the scalding mugs from palm to palm.

"Could you begin at the beginning and explain a bit?"

"How much do you know?"

"We know more or less everything, except what he's doing.

"And what everybody else is doing," added Nicky truthfully, "of course."

It had taken as long as this for the Master's age to sink into their minds.

"He *can't* be 157!" exclaimed Judy. "Can he?"

"He is."

"Jiminy!"

"It is a bit of a bind."

"Was he drunk?" asked Nicky, who had seen him.

"No."

"Nicky says he can't talk without whisky."

"Nicky is exactly right."

"Why?"

136

"He stopped talking English — or writing it for that matter — in 1900. After that the diaries are in Chinese for ten years and then it's a kind of shorthand with pictures. When he wants to say something in English, he has to paralyse his higher centres or whatever the doctors call the things. Drunk people start babbling, you know. He starts talking. English or Latin or anything. Anyway, he talks with the help of whisky."

"He said Non Omnis Something to me."

"Moriar. He once said it to me too. It means, 'I shall not wholly perish'."

"And what does that mean?"

"Successor," hissed Judy, thus scoring about ten out of ten for the evening's I.Q.

"Yes. He spotted you for pressing on with the work. That's what you are being educated for. So was I. So were the others. And also, of course, he needs people to help him — sort of staff jobs."

"But all I do is read about animals!"

"Biology, Anthropology, Pre-history, History, Psychology, Economics. In that order. Look at those."

On the shelf behind the plain iron bed was a row of books stretching from Spengler to Ouspenski.

Judy asked, "How does he talk actually?"

"It's a kind of thought transference. With the Chinaman it is. I can't do it. Look, I can't explain properly. He can read most people's minds as if they were speaking, and make them do things, too. But people differ. Judy was easy — you see, I've been told about you both — but Nicky was a stone wall. So was I once. So were the Chinaman and Totty, and poor old Pinkie most of all. He still can't hypnotize Pinkie."

"Can he hypnotize you?"

"I don't know. But he can tell what I am thinking."

"What about the Chinaman?"

"It is different for everybody. Those two can read each other's thoughts when they want to, but I don't know if he can influence the Chinaman's will. Totty was the weakest. In the end, he could use Totty like anybody else, and the poor devil tried to cheat him. To begin with, we were all stone walls like Nicky, and those are the kind of people he needs."

"I thought you couldn't hypnotize people against their will?"

"It isn't hypnotism, Judy, and it isn't thought reading. It's a real discovery like . . . well, like relativity, I suppose. You know how Einstein discovered that Space was curved. Well, Time is too, or Thought is, or something like that. Ordinary people wouldn't understand. But it is simple to him, and it is a fact. He got there about 1910. It has something to do with Time and Space being parts of the same thing."

"What does he want us for?"

"To help him conquer the world."

CHAPTER SEVENTEEN

Freedom of Choice

Mr. Frinton had begun to look exhausted and impatient as they talked. The strain of having worked himself up to do what he had been going to do, the danger and frustration of it, and now the effort to explain so many things to children, these had been working on his nerves in spite of his courtesy. A furtive, resentful, unfriendly expression began to dodge in his brown eyes — not because he was angry with them, but because he was angry with himself. He did not want to be unkind, but feared that he was going to be. He had no idea that the twins could be of any use — in fact, they were a crashing nuisance — and the quick change from assassin to nursery-maid had been another straw for the camel's back. His blue jowls began to have a hanging look and the balding head shone jaundiced in the electric light.

There was so much to explain, and it needed an effort.

He was a kind man with a conscience. Few people would have bothered with Nicky and Judy at a time like this, or been helpful about their puzzles. He had gone to kill the Master for reasons of his own, a mission of peril because of the powers involved, and he had realized that these powers must not be provoked while the children were there. He had been willing to risk his own life, but not theirs. They were a stumbling-block, in affairs much more important than those of kids, and he resented it. He was trying to remember that he must resent the situation, not them.

But I can't do anything tonight, he told himself. Poor little devils, they must be worried to death.

As a matter of fact, they were enthralled.

"Why does he want to do that?"

"Look, Nicky, I can't go into the whole thing. I'm tired. All that is . . ."

He flashed one of his apologetic smiles with an effort and ended, "Well, it's a question of faith and morals."

Judy was brooding on the main feature.

"I don't see how anybody can be 157."

"Well, I don't know," said Nicky. "He's only about fifty years older than that French revue actress."

"Which one?"

"The one Daddy talks about."

"Oh."

Pause.

"Do you suppose she could talk to him without speaking?"

"It would be pretty frightful," said Nicky earnestly, "wouldn't it?"

Mr. Frinton laughed out loud, saying, "Yes, all

about how La Goulue stole one of her songs to sing to King Edward the Seventh when he was Prince of Wales. The *Marseillaise*, I dare say."

He stopped laughing and added sombrely, "Do you realize that the *Marseillaise* really was a new song when he was born?"

"Are you sure it is true?"

"You only have to look at him."

"People were pretty old in the Bible."

"Not only in the Bible. Old Parr was supposed to be 152, but you can't verify it because there were no birth certificates in those days. Another chap called Henry Jenkins claimed to be 169. There was a Countess of Desmond who was said to have died by tumbling out of an apple tree when she was 140, and people generally do remember the birth dates of countesses. It's certain that her husband did die seventy years before she did."

"I wonder what it feels like?"

"I doubt if it feels like anything at all."

"Numb?"

"Not in his head."

"Why does he drink all that on Saturdays?"

"Nobody knows. I thought it might be something to do with the health of his mind. A sort of medicine."

"Like Epsom salts?"

"Why not?"

"Who is he, anyway?"

"Just an old man who was born ten years before Darwin. He was a country gentleman once, like your

father. Only he has gone on living and gone on thinking. It must be a lonely life."

"Why does he have to be murdered?"

"He has to be."

"Why?"

"People can't have dictators."

"Why not?"

"Because you have to be free to choose between
right and wrong."

"Even if you choose wrong?"

"I take it so."

Judy had been thinking hard and asked, "*Why* does
he want to conquer the world?"

"To rule it."

"Why?"

"Look at it."

"Little dost thou know, my son," remarked Nicky
suddenly, "with what a small store of wisdom the
world is governed."

"Exactly."

"If he did govern it, would it be better?"

"He says so."

"Would it?"

"Nicky, at present we have got people like President
Eisenhower and Sir Anthony Eden and Mr. Khruschev
or whoever it is, all armed with atomic bombs. Most
politicians can barely sign their own names or read a
comic strip. They are too busy winning elections to
educate themselves. They have to rant instead of
reading or growing up, but they have these weapons
all the same. Wouldn't you rather be organized by a

wise man of a hundred and a half, especially if there was only one of him doing it, instead of a competition between the ones we've got?"

"Yes, I would."

"That's what I used to believe. For one thing, it would unite the world."

"Then why do we want to kill him?"

Mr. Frinton looked more tired than ever and said, massaging his eye sockets, "He has been digging out this island for forty years."

"How do you mean?"

"Before the atomic bombs."

"If he was getting ready to be a dictator before it happened," explained Judy, "it was because he wanted to be one."

"He may have forseen it," said Mr. Frinton fairly. "We are like dogs talking about a human."

"Nicky said that too."

"I believed in him till a few days ago."

"What made you change your mind?"

"Nothing. It was changing all the time."

He went on to himself, clenching his fist, forgetting the listeners: "But I believe — this I must believe or perish — that we *have* to have freedom of choice. Evolution would stop without it. If monkeys can't choose to be men, if natural selection has no mutations to choose from, then we are stuck. The ants got stuck in dictatorship a hundred thousand years ago, and they have stayed the same ever since. Unless you have private enterprise and the freedom to choose wrong, you can't have progress."

CHAPTER EIGHTEEN

The Counter-Scanners

"IF you want to go to bed," said Judy gently, "we will go."

"No. Let's have it out. I have to fly to the mainland tomorrow."

"Why?"

"To fetch things. And to keep out of the way."

"Is he after you too, like Dr. McTurk?"

"He might be."

"Then please don't come back."

"I am only operational when I'm here. Besides, what about you?

"Don't worry," he added. "I keep away as much as I can for fear of a brainwashing, that's all. It's one of those things. It's a piece of cake."

He was seeing his peril. That was why he slipped into the slang of older dangers.

"How is he going to conquer the world?"

"It is with these vibrator jobs."

"Please will you tell us about them?"

"I would if I could. You would have to be a radar expert to understand — even the beginning part.

"And," he said wearily, "I suppose you'd have to be a hundred and fifty to understand the end."

"How do they work?"

"It has something to do with frequencies. Everything has a vibration of its own, they tell me, and the vibrator units can interfere with it. You know those huge cup-shaped things they build in Alaska, to take in the radar waves? Well, these little ones do it backwards. They send them out."

"What happens then?"

"At the exact pitch, they stop things vibrating."

"What happens when you stop vibrating?"

"You stop."

He peered into his cocoa mug grimly, sloshing the cold dregs round the side.

"This island," he said, "is nicely half way between Russia and America. He didn't choose it only because it was lonely. If the vibrators point outwards in a ring, he can blow a sort of bubble of counter-pitch round us. He can make it bigger or smaller. He could expand it round the world.

"Think of a soap bubble floating in your bath. If you had an air tube at its centre in Rockall, you could blow it higher and wider, round the tube. In the end, it would fill the bath. If the bath was rounded like the world, the bubble would meet itself at the other side, eight thousand miles under our feet — at Midway Island or somewhere."

"How do you mean stop?"

"Stop being."

145

He added, wondering whether he ought to say so, "There was nothing of Totty left to bury."

"Would the world vanish?"

"I really don't know. It would be inert anyway. What does happen when things have no frequency?"

"But that would be the end of everything."

"He couldn't rule the world," explained Judy, "if it wasn't there."

"Yes, but he doesn't have to use them at the exact pitch. If the frequency is a fraction off beat, things just tend to seize up. Besides, the bubble needn't be sent right round. Think what would happen if he blew an off-beat bubble which reached from Newfoundland to Moscow and Spitzbergen to Liberia."

"What would happen?"

"I suppose he could say to President Eisenhower and Mr. Khrushchev: 'Look, everybody in England and France and Spain and Germany has a hell of a headache, all their machinery has gone dead, unless you surrender to me I will expand my bubble.'"

"How would he say it?"

"Broadcast, I suppose."

"Then they would have to pack in."

"Or try the headache, worse and worse."

"But suppose they sent an atomic bomb for him, in a guided missile or something?"

"It would fall to bits when it reached the bubble."
"Well!"

"How soon," asked Nicky, "is all this going to happen?"

"Now."

"But . . ."

"Everything is ready, except for the details. It could be next week. I have to collect some vanadium wire for one more vibrator on the next trip."

"And you were working for this man!"

"I did, Judy. You see, I believe in a single government for the world."

"Even then I don't see how half a dozen people could govern it. I mean, there must be such a lot of things to look after."

"He would keep on the present staff, probably. He would only have to fix their brains, like the engineers and the trawler crew."

"Then what's the use of you and the Chinaman and Nicky?"

He passed his hands over his eyes again, still more tired.

"Partly to make the things — for instance Pinkie and Totty and the Chinaman. Partly to manage supplies, for instance me. Partly as bodyguards, I dare say, when the time comes. Partly secretaries. Partly as unsuggestible people, except where he's concerned. And partly to carry on when he dies. He will die, you know. He isn't immortal or supernatural. He is a real man, except he has that age and brain. I must remember he is only real.

He added firmly, "And can be put away."

Judy asked nervously, "Are you really going to bring the vanadium?"

"I might be able to put it off. I could say it was not delivered."

"If you don't do it sooner or later, will he do what he did to the Doctor?"

"He might have a bash at it."

While they were considering this, he explained, "That isn't the point. He could probably make do with what he has already. I can't stay away or warn people or refuse to deliver."

"Why not?"

"Such a lot of questions."

"We are sorry."

"Look, honeys, there are lots of answers. He has enough to start with, so it's too late. Even if it wasn't too late, nobody would believe me on the other side. Can you see a broken-down Squadron-Leader asking for an interview with President Eisenhower to tell him our story without proof, at this time of day? And also he has found out how to read my mind — and to make me do things, I think — if I am within sight. Do you realize that every time I am called to the boudoir I have to make my brain a blank — if I can? It's an agony, like praying. I don't even know if I'm getting away with it . . . or whether he's just not attending . . . If he attended for a moment. . . ."

His head went between his hands for the third time.

"And oh!' cried Nicky. "This place is wired for sound!"

Mr. Frinton said to the floor, "No, it isn't. That's a sort of tannoy, and it doesn't play back."

"The Doctor thought it was wired."

"He was a fool."

After a pause, he lifted a face of exhaustion, saying:

"Why should he bother to wire for sound when he only has to look at us? Don't you realize that he could tell what everybody is thinking or saying or has thought or has said, merely by looking at any person except Nicky?"

CHAPTER NINETEEN

The Chinaman

Judy came out of the sea next morning, gleaming like a seal. They had forgotten about the Master.

She exclaimed in triumph, "Supersonic-whiz-bang-pop! And there's nobody to scandalize!"

They had coaxed a rope from the engineers. It could be fixed on the slanting side of the island, where the yacht's boat had first landed. Holding this, or not swimming far from it, it was possible to bathe on calm days without being swept away by the dangerous currents of Rockall.

Jokey, who knew how to look after number one, padded uneasily along the steep waterline, sometimes lifting one paw and whimpering for them to come out. She had no intention of having another bath night. She was not a believer in dogs who sit by the graves of their masters until they pine away. She believed in *survival*, not sea-bathing or pining, and if anybody had to be drowned, who intended to be the survivor but Jokey?

Judy's reference to scandal was because they had no clothes on. Not having been warned that they were going to be kidnapped, they had not brought the necessities of life — like frogman flippers and bathers — so they had to swim bare.

They clambered out by the aid of the rope, slashing the water on the hot granite, and lay spreadeagle to dry. They were brown all over. They had even peeled on their undersides, for instance under their eyebrows or their noses, because the sun bounced upwards from the burnished surface of the sea and might have given them sunstroke even with hats on — except that they were used to it. When they smiled, the coffee-coloured faces suddenly split open with a gash like bleached melon seeds, giving them a slightly mad expression, like cannibals. Only their eyeballs and their teeth were white. They might have rolled the one and eaten you with the other — singing *Darkies Sing A Happy Song* or something of that sort.

Their satin skins tasted of salt, which had helped the sunburn. They filled these skins like pythons. The shadows of the smooth muscles were faintly violet as they slid.

The molten sea stretched away to infinity. The inside of their eyelids, closed against the gong of the sun, was a salmon-coloured curtain with solar systems moving in it.

"If," said Nicky, "we had our overalls, you could sew them."

"So could you."

"Women expect men to mend cars. Why shouldn't men expect women to mend trousers?"

"Wah, wah, wah!"

"That isn't an answer."

"Ask of the winds that strew around their something on the something."

"Is that a quotation?"

"Yes."

'What from?"

"I can't remember."

"Anyway," added Judy, "it's probably wrong. It might be 'waves'."

"Ask of the something that strew around their something on the something. Yes, that's much clearer."

"Sarky parky sat in the Arky . . . "

"What do you think that means?"

"It's extempore."

"Ex what?"

"Ha, Ha!" said Judy. "One thing our little lecturer doesn't know."

"We forgot to ask him about Pinky's tongue."

"I didn't. There were a lot of things I remembered to ask him, but you can't ask everything at once."

"Judy remembers everything."

"Everything," she said, taking up a hopeless position.

"Do you remember when the world was made?"

"You can't remember something when you weren't there."

"Then do you remember . . . remember . . . remember what the square of seven thousand and three was?"

"Yes, I do."

"What?"

"Five."

"Judy!"

"Well, what was it then?"

That had him.

"It couldn't be five anyway, because . . ."

She began to sing, "Seventy sevens make ninety-nine on a cold and frosty morning."

"I suppose that's extemporary too."

"One of the things we forgot to ask was why the Doctor knew."

"The square of a number . . ."

"Oh, Jokey, do get off my tummy. You don't *know* how sharp your claws are."

"Another thing we never asked was anything at all about the Chinaman."

The Chinaman, who had been standing on a ledge behind and above them, unseen because their eyes were shut, said, "Why not ask him now?"

Judy shot up like a jack-knife and reached for her nightshirt.

Nicky said, "I'm sorry."

They scrambled into their clothes, the sleeves dangling and the touselled hair jamming in the collars, making the attitudes of scarecrows.

"Thank you," said Judy, from inside her tangle, "for the magic china.

She emerged to add, "It was really lovely."

"I am glad."

He sat down on the rock beside them. They looked at him for almost the first time, as if he were a person. He had been too strange before — too much mixed up with automatic pistols and darksome deeds and

Chinese finger nails. He had left these off, they saw, and was dressed in a white laboratory coat instead of his dragon gown. He was in his working clothes. It is an odd fact that when people shoot at you, you often forgive them and forget about it — provided they miss. It seems as if the mind prefers not to remember its dangers, or else it would be in a dither all the time.

They noticed that he was not like a stage Chinaman out of Sax Romer after all. He did not have a pigtail — nor one of those long thin moustaches hanging down to his chest — and his eyes were not particularly slanting. When his face was in repose they did slant a little, like puffy buttonholes with a twist at the outer edges, but when he was trying to look European, as he was now, he kept them wide open on purpose — which corrected the angle. And when he smiled, as he was doing also, the smooth, meaty face burst into a hundred jovial folds or dimples, full of benevolence. His plump, soft hands lived a private life of their own, gently massaging and reassuring one another.

"How does the jug warble?"

"Ah ha!" said he. "But will you not like it better if you never know?"

"Nicky says there must be tubes inside which make air-locks — like when the water pipes bumble in a heating system."

He made a polite, hissing sound, to show his admiration for Nicky's cleverness. But he did not tell them.

"Had you been listening for long?"

"I heard you wondering about the blackamoor and the Chinaman."

"We didn't mean to be rude."

"I am sure of it."

"*Would* you tell us about Pinkie?"

"Why not? There is nothing to conceal.

"Besides," he added, bowing and twinkling, "you have evidently been cross-examining my colleague the Squadron-Leader. A delightful fellar."

He said "fellar" in the Edwardian way, like the Duke. His beautiful English was idiomatic with the faintest tinge of being the wrong idiom — not from the accent but because it was out of date.

"*Did* they cut out his tongue?"

"I am sorry to say, Yes."

"Why?"

(Judy said, "How beastly!")

"You must remember that the Master has been making his arrangements for many years. He has of course developed."

"How do you mean?"

"You should find out the seniority of his lieutenants upon our island."

Since they hardly liked to say "Well?" or "What about it?" he went on. "The blackamoor is our oldest inhabitant, senior to me. He was an artisan from the beginning, and not suggestible."

"Do you mean he had to be made into a mute because he couldn't be mesmerized?"

"He is a simple creature. He does not resent it. He is quite happy."

"But to cut out his tongue!"

"Freud says somewhere or other: 'Conflicts of

interests among human beings are principally decided by the application of violence.' "

"Do you mean that he is like Nicky and can't be made to do things — or forget?"

"That is so. Partly so."

"Why only partly?"

"When the negro was silenced in 1920, the Master had not developed his control of mind to its present pitch. Oddly enough — perhaps because of a different racial background — it still remains a fact that Pinkie cannot be influenced. So the operation has justified itself after all! On the other hand, you must not feel too certain that Nicholas is beyond his reach. In difficult cases, the Master is always probing for the proper contact and — except for the blackamoor — he has generally reached it in one degree or another. Mr. Frinton and I and the unlucky Doctor were also 'hard nuts to crack'."

"Can he mesmerize you?"

"For different people the extent of control is different."

"Poor Pinkie!"

"You need not disturb yourself about him, Miss Judith. He is contented and is a master craftsman. He enjoys making things. Without his nimble fingers, our simple instruments would never be constructed."

"So he is being kept for that?"

"Just as the Doctor was kept."

Nicky suddenly asked, "Have some people not been kept?"

There was no bid for the answer.

"What was the Doctor kept for?"

"Surely you must have guessed?"

"We don't think he was a very good doctor."

"He was our calculating machine. Human beings are often born as mathematical freaks, and sometimes they can earn their living by answering dates and things of that sort on the music halls. They take up less space than electronic brains, are less liable to break down, often quicker, need less upkeep, and are generally stupid people in other respects. He was invaluable while the calculations lasted. Luckily, they had been finished before he became unserviceable."

"What did he want to do?"

"He wanted to take over from the Master."

"So I suppose," said Judy thoughtfully, "that everybody here is kept for use, or not at all?"

"Precisely so."

"What use are we?"

"Apart from the mental advantages of Master Nicholas as a successor, your father and your uncle will be of real help in future negotiations on a government level. They are distinguished people."

"And Mr. Frinton?"

"Transport. Unfortunately, it is impossible to fly an aircraft on theory — particularly for sedentary gentlemen who are more than a century and a half old."

Nicky's mind went off at a tangent.

"Why do you have the trawler? Surely there is a way of making fresh water nowadays, and isn't it better to have as few people as possible?"

"Fuel. Heavy machinery. Besides, their minds are blank."

"Blank?"

"It might be more accurate to say, convinced."

"Convinced of what?"

"The human mind can be convinced of almost anything. The lunatic asylums of England are full of people who are convinced they are tea-pots. They are not lying when they tell you so and they have no need to deceive. These men of ours are convinced that they are trawling."

"Then that leaves you."

"My services are linguistic, in a humble way."

"We don't understand."

"The Chinese language, Miss Judith, is not based on nouns and verbs. Thus it is not based on Space and Time, Matter and Mind, or the other dualisms which involve the concepts of Mass and Motion. At the turn of the century, the Master found that it was no longer possible to express his mental processes in English, so he cast about for an alternative way. Chinese proved useful for the time being — though we have since developed our better means of communication."

"If you don't talk Chinese any more," said Nicky bitterly, "I should have thought he wouldn't have kept you."

"I have made myself useful in the laboratory."

The birds of Rockall, which they had been watching out of the corner of one eye — because they always did watch birds — seemed strangely different from the world in which they found themselves. A small, black and white Razorbill went whirring past, banked swiftly by using its feet as rudders, and landed on the sea with a splash. When there was no wind, the sea birds took off and landed less gracefully than usual. It floated there like a cork, buoyant as an egg-shell or a phalarope, then suddenly ducked. First it was there, then, with a definite header, not there. It was out of sight, swimming down in a trail of bubbles, flying with its wings under water, in pursuit of fish. They hardly noticed it.

"How did the Master get hold of all these people in the first place?"

"By advertisement. Mr. Frinton, for example, answered an advertisement in *The Times* newspaper, and I interviewed him in Belfast."

"I suppose you simply advertised for a pilot?"

"He was at a loose end after the second war, having been taught no skills except to kill his neighbour. Smuggling, you know, and the sale of aircraft to Israel. A minor operative."

"We think Mr. Frinton is a nice man, and we believe what he tells us."

"A delightful chap."

"Are you on his side or the Master's?"

The Chinaman thought.

He said carefully, "You will understand that any form of intimacy or cabal is difficult in a situation where minds are open to be inspected."

"Do you do everything that the Master tells you?"

With a blank, gamboge coloured face, but taking his life in his hands, he answered softly, looking at the rock between his feet, "No."

"I knew he didn't," said Judy. "He wouldn't have given us the Nightingale if he hadn't been friends."

"And pushing us off the cliff?"

He explained, "I am under orders."

"So when you are told to shoot at children," said Nicky, "you do."

"If you will consider the facts which you have gathered from Mr. Frinton and myself, perhaps you will see that our position is not an easy one. In the presence of the Master I am seldom 'my own man'."

They fell silent, each thinking a different thought.

The Razorbill came up from one of his plunges, glancing over his shoulder, shaking his head. He was so close that they could see the white stripe on his bill, like the ring on an officer's sleeve. He also had a bar on his wing.

The Chinaman was thinking, *No, I will not press them further for the time being.*

CHAPTER TWENTY

Sunrise on Wednesday

JOKEY was fairly happy wherever the twins were, but she had a secret sorrow. Most of the food on the island was tinned — which she did not like — and her favourite of all dishes was unobtainable. This dish was kippers. On Wednesday mornings at Gaunt's God-stone, the day after the fishmonger called, there were always kippers for breakfast. It had made the day into a Red-Letter one for her, on which she based her week. Without kippers, there were no Wednesdays. It upset the calendar, as if she were a clergyman after Sunday had been abolished.

It was Wednesday now, and Jokey woke up early. She woke from a dream of dustbins, stuffed to the brim with comb-like kipper bones — the tail left on at the back, like the propeller of a toy aeroplane, and the ghastly, golden head in front, goggle-eyed and pouting. She woke with the divine smell in her nostrils, thinking: If I should die think only this of me that there's some corner of a foreign isle that is for ever kippers.

It was all very well for the children, who were young and adaptable. They had settled down on the island more or less, as though they really were having a holiday, in spite of the situation. They splashed about in the lovely ocean or explored the wonders of the engine room, endless to Nicky, while the friendly greasers gossiped about football pools, which could be followed on the wireless. But Jokey was growing elderly, by the standards of dogs. She was missing other things besides kippers — the kind of things that elderly people do miss, their own particular chair to sit on by the fire, their cronies like the setter Sherry who belonged to the Duchess, and even the kitchen cat. She did not care for changes of scene, for strange islands where there were no rabbits, but birds instead, which bit you horribly. Her nose was sore. She was haunted by the vague suspicion that somebody might at any moment pop out from somewhere and push her in the sea. A believer in personal survival, she resented this. Her kippers had vanished. There was no grass to eat when she wanted to be sick. Insecurity and the lack of home comforts had begun to sour an outlook on human reliability which had never been rosy, except where the twins were concerned.

She walked along Judy's bed and put one paw in the girl's eye, to wake her up. She knew that people who were awake had their eyes open and this simple process, like pushing back the lid of a slot machine, was effective.

"Jokey!"

It was about four o'clock in the morning when they stumbled into the open air, rubbing their gummy eyelids, on the theory that Jokey needed to do her business — which she didn't.

The sun was up already. Or was it? In those latitudes, the short summer night ended with such a long-drawn break of day that it was difficult to tell the exact moment.

They stood in the windless calm of morning, still a bit chilly in their nightshirts from the warm beds they had left behind them, while the opal, milky, silent sea — it was going to be a scorching day and on the mainland there must have been a misty dew — while the sea merged into the colourless sky without a line between them. Presently, as Jokey pottered about and the seabirds, busy already, flew and fished perhaps a little drowsily, the faintest traces of carmine and cadmium yellow began to suggest themselves in the ghostly dome of sunrise, tender and delicate like the sheen of feathers on a pigeon's neck. The sun, soon to be tyrannous, was floating tranquilly within the fog of dayspring. The birds of ocean, just like the birds of woodland England, became vociferous. In Gaunt's Godstone, at dawn, the birdsong sometimes throbbed in waves of sound, like somebody fiercely pulsing on a concertina with his finger on the stop which prevents the notes from playing. Here, in the sea, the noise was like a holiday from a lunatic asylum.

"How lovely it is to be awake."

She purposely did not say "before other people". She did not mean that they had the sunrise to themselves. She only felt that it was better to be alive than dead.

"Jokey is shamming. Let's see if we can make some breakfast."

The big, white kitchen was empty and tidy. It was living its secret life without people, just as it did every night after they had gone to bed.

They found fruit-juice in the refrigerator, with tins of milk and cereals and coffee in other places. Jokey sniffed gloomily at the doors, confirming the absence of her delicacy. Like the people who were worried by the change of calendar in the eighteenth century, she felt like marching about with a placard saying, "Give Us Our Eleven Days (kippers)." She disapproved of progress.

Nicky said, waking up with the lovely warmth and morning aroma of coffee, "Because a person gives you a trilling jug, it doesn't mean you have to trust him."

"He told us the truth. Everything fits in with what Mr. Frinton said."

"For that matter, why should you trust Mr. Frinton? They may be in league."

"Do you?"

"Well, I suppose I do."

"You see."

"I don't think people start killing each other because they . . . sort of disapprove of each other's principles."

"People like Mr. Frinton might."

"Why?"

"Well, he is a serious man."

"I expect he killed a lot of people in the war too," added Judy.

"But why does he have to *kill* the Master? Couldn't he lock him up or break his vibrators or something?"

"He would always be there to start again. Besides,

with the mesmerism and stuff, how would he get at him?"

"How was he going to shoot him, then?"

"Perhaps he could pop round the door and fire before the mesmerizing worked?"

"He didn't seem very certain about it."

"In any case, it isn't just principles," said Judy. "The Master has done things. We don't even know how many things. He could be hanged for the Doctor."

"What *are* the principles?" asked Nicky.

She was more interested in Mr. Frinton's nature.

"He has been more or less kidnapped himself. With the mesmerizing. He has got to get free. Besides, think of Pinkie's tongue."

"All the same, it would be a good idea to unite the world, wouldn't it? If there were no separate countries, they couldn't go to war with each other."

"No."

"One of them said — yes, the Doctor said — that you sometimes had to kill a few people to save a great many. He said it was the scientific attitude."

"That's why Mr. Frinton has to kill the Master."

"All this killing," said Nicky disgustedly, "it's like being in a film. Why can't people behave sensibly?"

"They don't."

"Why can't we just say the Master's idea is a jolly good one, and let it go?"

"You can't make people be good by force."

"They do us," he said gloomily. "With a hair brush."

"But . . ."

"It seems to me," said Nicky, "that everything is in a muddle. If . . ."

"Look," said the practical Judy. "Do you approve of being spanked?"

"No, I don't."

"Well, then."

"Well, then what?"

"If you can't make people be good with a hair brush, you can't with a vibrator, can you?"

"I don't think it is the same."

"It is the same," said Judy, "and besides, Mr. Frinton is nice. That's the real point."

"If he is all that nice," he said, seeing round a corner, "and disapproves of hair brushes, why does he want to spank the Master? Because that's what it comes to. He would be using force himself."

Judy said doggedly, "Mr. Frinton is nice."

As a matter of fact, there was nothing else to say — except what the Squadron-Leader had himself said, that the scheme had been started before the bombs had been discovered. And there was the need for mutations.

"Life seems pretty difficult."

"What we began on was the Chinaman."

"I don't think he cares a bit about principles, and I don't believe in him like in Mr. Frinton. He said that thing about violence. Which is force."

"I suppose you can stop a lot of force by using a little."

"Even then, I don't trust him."

"He has trusted us."

"How?"

"By telling things which were true. Think how dangerous it was for him to say that he did not always obey the Master."

"He might be getting at something."

"What?"

"He might be trying to trap us."

"What for?"

"I don't know."

"Nicky, why not ask him?"

"We might."

"We have asked other things, and he didn't mind. He did almost say that he was on the same side as Mr. Frinton."

"He was being careful."

"Don't you see how he has to be? Why don't we ask him to help Mr. Frinton straight out? Then there would be two of them. If the Master can see into their minds, they wouldn't have dared to confide things to each other, but we know now, and we could bring them together."

"How much does he see into minds?"

"So far as I can make out, it is most into people like me and least into people like Pinkie, and the others are between the two. Probably the Chinaman is harder than Mr. Frinton."

"Ju, I don't think it's much good interfering. We are only twelve."

"Well, if you want to sit and suck your thumb . . ."

"It isn't that. It's this mesmerizing stuff."

"He said it wasn't mesmerizing. He said it was a

real thing like Relativity, and then there was all that
about Mind and Matter, which the Chinaman said."

"Suppose Mr. Frinton didn't want us to tell the
Chinaman?"

"We could sound him out, without telling."

"I wonder what he's called?"

"Oh, it will be Mo or Wu or something. It doesn't
matter."

"If Mr. Frinton wanted him to know, he would
have told him himself."

"But he may not have guessed he was friendly. We
may be the only people who have had a hint."

"How do you know?"

"He would have told us otherwise."

"I suppose it is sensible?"

"We don't need to tell the Chinaman about Mr.
Frinton's plan, Nicky, not right out. We can be tactful
and sort of talk round it. Then, if he catches on, there
will be more people on our side."

"So long as we don't give anything away."

"Imagine if they could work together! Probably
they have both been planning to stop the Master,
without either of them knowing it."

"Give Jokey some milk," said Nicky uncomfortably
— thus agreeing to press upon the Chinaman exactly
what he wanted to press on them.

CHAPTER TWENTY-ONE

Golden Tiger

THEY discovered, to their astonishment, that his name was Mr. Blenkinsop. "My real name," he explained, "means Golden Tiger in the Tea Forest, but I could hardly expect my friends in Europe to call me that. Rather than suffer the annoyance of mispronunciation, I changed it to Blenkinsop when I went to Oxford, by deed poll. No, I am not deceiving you like Dr. Totty. Blenkinsop is a distinctive surname, which has the advantage of being easily remembered. Look, I have brought Miss Judith a little gift. No, please. I beg you not to mention it. I have several ornaments of an oriental nature in my bedroom on the private side and it can well be spared. One day you must come to see the others."

It was a superb papier-mâché tiger, done in red and orange stripes, nearly as big as Jokey. Its head and tail were on springs inside, so that, by jogging them, it could be made to nod and wag in a way that was partly fearsome and partly comical. The fearsome parts were its stripes and whiskers — rather like a cat-fish — but the nodding made it clear that it was only

pretending to be desperate. Judy felt at once that it
ought to be given a ball of wool to play with, growling
and letting on to be fierce, but Nicky was more taken
by its fearful symmetry. The technical name for it was
an Amoy Cat.

"You see, it is a Golden Tiger like myself. I hope
you will be fond of it."

"It is glorious. I don't think we ought to have it."

"You will do me a favour by accepting."

"If you can really spare it. . . ."

Nicky said, "Try it on Jokey."

They did, but on the whole it was a flop. If it had
smelt of tigers, the result would have been different.
As it didn't, she watched it nodding for a little with a
dubious expression, then sat down vulgarly and began
to bite her tail.

Mr. Blenkinsop was not disconcerted. He examined
the small dog with an unreadable expression, his eyes
like two poached eggs with one thin slit across the
outer skin.

"The Pekinese," he said thoughtfully, "which is
the comforter of my own nation, is said to be descended
from the Lion and the Butterfly. Some say the Lion and
the Marmoset. They fell in love, and the result was
the Pekinese. The smaller ones were carried about
by the ladies of the court, inside their sleeves, like foot
warmers or muffs."

"Darling Jokey, would you like to be a muff?"

"She would make a better bottle brush," said Nicky.

"How could you!"

"A fashionable hostess once said to me, while she

was praising one of our imperial dogs, 'Oh, if only it was skinned, it would make me such a beautiful tippet.' I replied 'My dear lady, if only you were skinned, you would make me a beautiful pair of boots.' "

They looked at him, stunned. He was human! From that moment, they began to feel that they could have no doubts of Mr. Blenkinsop, if he liked dogs. It was what he had wanted them to feel.

"What did she say?"

"She went away in a huff."

"And a muff!" cried Nicky, idiotically pleased. They rolled about with Jokey, nearly squashing the tiger, shouting "Huff" and "Muff" and "Wuff"!

"Can we go and see your other ornaments?"

"Some time when the Master is busy."

"Doesn't he want us to come on the private side?"

"It is inconvenient."

By mentioning Him, they had damped their spirits.

"Could we come when he is drunk on Saturday?"

"He is never drunk."

"Mr. Blenkinsop," said Judy tactfully, "don't you think he ought to be stopped?"

"It had 'crossed my mind'."

"Why do you help him?"

"For the same reasons as your friend the Squadron-Leader."

"Mr. Frinton says . . ."

Nicky coughed hard, but she went on firmly,

"He says that people ought to be free to choose between right and wrong."

"It is a point of view."

"Do you believe in it?"

"Mr. Frinton's 'heart is in the right place.'"

"I knew you would!"

Nicky had gone off abruptly on one of his wool-gathering expeditions.

"It has something to do with vivisection," he explained.

"What has?"

"Killing few for many."

This struck Judy as a good point of re-entry for tact.

"Do you believe in vivisection, Mr. Blenkinsop?"

He had the wit to say, "No."

"You see, you can't do it to things that trust you. Nicky says he would do it to things that don't trust, like cats I suppose, but you can't betray anything that believes in you. You just can't. Not monkeys, not dogs, not horses. . . .

"As a matter of fact, not anything trustful. Pigs are lovely really and we once brought up a lamb. . . . Oh, Mr. Blenkinsop, we ought to be vegetarians really, if only we were decent, but it's so dreadfully difficult for everybody, and we try not to think, but you do agree, don't you?"

Nicky said with careful thought, "If you betray things, you are hurting yourself. I think it does you more harm to die of treachery than to die of cancer because you didn't do it."

"Didn't do vivisection, he means."

"It is worse to kill your heart."

The Chinese hands were stroking and consoling each other.

"Would you cut up a man, Master Nicholas?"

"If he didn't trust me, I would."

"They can look after themselves," said Judy, "anyway."

"Would you cut up the Master?"

"That . . ." began Nicky, but this time it was his sister who trod on his toe. He glared at her.

"Mr. Frinton says. . . ."

"The point is," said Judy, "that Mr. Blenkinsop thinks he ought to be stopped."

"And how would you do that, Miss Judith?"

"Mr. Frinton," said Nicky straight out, "was going to shoot him."

They waited, half in horror at what they had said.

"Very interesting."

"Promise not to tell anybody?"

"It was all right to tell you, Mr. Blenkinsop, wasn't it? I mean, you did say . . ."

"You had better explain to me about it."

"We oughtn't to. We can't. Only if . . ."

"Your secret is safe with me."

"Swear?"

He swore with impassive solemnity, lifting one hand in the air without looking ridiculous, while they examined him anxiously. There is no art, as Shakespeare said, to find the mind's construction in the face — particularly not in an oriental one. They told him everything.

"Mr. Frinton," he said at the end, "is an impulsive young gentleman."

They waited.

"The position is more difficult than he thinks."

"But you will help?"

The cosy hands stopped fondling and spread themselves palm downwards while he shrugged.

"I can be of no assistance."

"But you said . . ."

"Listen, Miss Judith, you must try to understand about what you call the Master's mesmerism. He is not a superhuman being, but he is our master after all. And he is this because he has explored two lines of investigation further than most people have done. He is a hypnotist, but there are many of these. There is nothing unusual about his mental suggestions, except, perhaps, the extent to which he has developed them. The other line is extrasensory perception. It has long been recognized that space is not separate from time. The world of physics is a space-time world. They are two aspects of the same thing. It is impossible for me to explain to you in the language of nouns and verbs — since the very words 'mind' and 'matter' are themselves nouns — how the world of extrasensory perception is a mind-matter world, again two aspects of the same thing. I trust you are understanding some part of what I say?"

"Go on."

"The Master has taught himself to operate in a mind-matter continuum which renders Mr. Frinton's revolver derisory."

"Do you mean it wouldn't go off?"

"Nothing so stupid. Mr. Frinton would not fire it off."

"We thought he might sort of pop round the door. . . ."

"The extent of the continuum varies with the individual. In the case of Mr. Frinton, he would probably be within the Master's consciousness the moment he entered the private side and he would do whatever the Master wanted him to do the moment he was within sight."

"Do you think he knew we were on the stairs?"

"Why not?"

"But he didn't do anything."

"There was no need to do anything."

Nicky was an imitative boy, or rather, he caught things from the people he admired. Now he put his head in his hands with puzzlement, like the Squadron-Leader.

"How much are you in this continuing thing?"

"I have for a long time been associated with the Master's investigations."

"But how much?"

Mr. Blenkinsop took a deep breath and closed his eyes. Even the slits vanished.

"By a mental effort," he said slowly, "which is an exhausting one, I am able to present a blank mind to my master, a mind partly erased by the dictation of my own consciousness. I am not able to resist his will if I am within sight of him."

"If you went to shoot him yourself," said Judy,

"I suppose he could will you not to pull the trigger quicker than you could pull it."

"But if you crept in," said Nicky, "if his back was turned?"

"The Master's back is never turned. He is conscious of my presence a little beyond the range of sight."

"You could erase your mind, or whatever it is."

"I should then have erased the pistol."

CHAPTER TWENTY-TWO

It Has Begun

THE Squadron-Leader was peering about in his cockpit with a nodding motion, like a hen pecking. Pilots, in their world of silence enclosed by the goldfish bowl of sound, have a secrecy and remoteness when seen from outside. What are they doing? What are they thinking? It is like eavesdropping to fly beside them, while their heads bob about and their hands occasionally do something, which could be anything from filling in crossword puzzles to picking their noses.

Mr. Frinton was fussing slightly about his navigation. If Rockall had not been forced to maintain a radio silence, finding it would have been what he called "a piece of cake". As it was, he had to navigate — which is slightly more difficult in helicopters, because of their crabbing. The machine had a service ceiling of about ten thousand feet, which meant that on a clear day he would in theory see more than a hundred miles. The summer haze restricted this a great deal, and he was at seven thousand anyway, which was more economical for fuel. You were supposed to see 93.1 miles at 5000 feet in clear atmospheres which never existed — and besides, see what? See a pin? In good weather, he decided, if you were very lucky, you might notice the island at twenty or thirty miles. He sat in the noise and vibration, which reminded him of old-fashioned open-cockpit types, blinking a little from the flicker effect of the rotor blades, doing the usual mental arithmetic about knots and winds and fuel consumption and compass bearings. At the same time, his mind was occupied with the Rockall problem of stopping the Master and evacuating the children, while his eye — which was, though he did not think so, that of a poet and an artist — ranged about automatically, from the instruments to the sea to the sky.

Outside the perspex, it was an opal evening, with no horizon. The dove-coloured haze and the flamingo cumulus clouds at his own level joined with the ocean, without a line between. He pondered about the levels of life. His air-fish floated and laboured in the lofty shade, as the sea-fish floated far below him, while on the surface a toad of a trawler forged steadily along, trailing its frog-legs of a wake. They were all in the same aquarium.

He noticed that the regular herringbone pattern of the waves did not fit with the surf of the white-caps. That is to say, there were no regular lines of foam in arcs or ranks, as there would be on a beach. Instead, the sea-flowers disclosed themselves irregularly, scattered here and there over the neat remote corrugation. Surf, he wondered? Scurf? Yes, it was like dandruff on the flat, grey coat of sea, seven thousand feet below the determined fuselage. Or a few vague flakes of snow on warming fur.

Meanwhile, Rockall was no bigger than the lump of Ortac in the English Channel, and he had to find it.

To come in at dusk, he thought. I wish I was flying to London Airport. Then, as the humming aerofoil bored steadfastly into the twilight, I should cross the lace skirts of the coast and see the bunkers of the golf courses, exactly like the impressions of a thumb-nail, and I would see the old scars of war-time bombing — moon-craters of dead tissue on the vast, darkling, homely, patterned, populated flesh of England. Yes, and the motor cars, crawling beetles on the map-like road, would be switching on their side-lights, and over London, in the darkness, the myriad streets would swing like the spokes of a wheel, all lighted. The window lights, the whole unending hive, would twinkle. It is because — he thought — each fore-ground chimney passes across each background window, as the aircraft bee-lines past, and this makes a flicker of interceptions. They really do twinkle.

How to get rid of the children, with so little time?

An attempt on the Master might end in anything — in the destruction of the island, for that matter. When a scientific maniac got control of things like atomic power it was only a matter of time before he destroyed the world. If Hitler had had it, for instance, would he not have abolished the planet as a funeral pyre, instead of merely pouring petrol over himself outside his bunker? The minds of tyrants seemed to work on the lines of "After Me the Deluge". Apart from that, many scientists were unbalanced. What Totty used to call the Scientific Attitude often resulted in cold, mad, dispassionate curiosity. They infected their own bodies with new-found serums and poisons and cure-alls, not because of selfless devotion to the good of the race, but because they were inquisitive or even masochistic. From *What Will Happen if I Give Myself An Injection of Xylocaine?* to *What Will Happen If I Let Off The Super-Bomb?*, was a small step.

If you interfered with the Master unsuccessfully, he might turn the vibrators inwards — or outwards, for that matter, at full strength. The thing was a frightful risk.

Bang on, he thought with satisfaction! There it was on the port side, black and lonely and minute against the reddening sea.

"Red sky at night, shepherd's delight."

He eased the collective-pitch lever with his left hand and moved the cyclic stick forward, increasing his speed from seventy-five to eighty knots as the machine descended. The island grew slowly as the height fell off, each of the two who were pledged at the rendezvous altering in size and position, not in speed or motion.

He circled, noting the arrow of the anemometer, looking for the lee-side, and turned into wind. His left hand lowered the collective-pitch lever further still, turning the throttle which was on the end of it, inwards, to decrease his power, while the right hand came back on the cyclic stick. All the time, and for every motion of the other controls, his feet lived a private life of their own on the anti-torque pedals, forgotten by the rest of the body.

It Has Begun

The drill went into reverse as the contraption sank, the lever now coming up and the stick forward, then into the reverse of reverse, balancing stability between the one and the other.

He came to the hover at ten feet.

He pushed the lever down until she settled, twisted its grip right inwards to throttle off, folded both hands for a moment in his lap, and sighed.

All switches off.

Oil cut-off, off.

Engine cooling shutters, open.

Directional gyro, caged.

Fuel cock, off.

He was there.

When the helicopter had been stowed and a written report delivered for the Master, Mr. Frinton handed himself over to Pinkie, who had been there to meet him as usual — and who had been greeted, as usual, with the friendly tease which pleased him, "How's the blackamoor?" He was hurried down the elevator and the kitchen passage to have his dinner.

In the kitchen, the twins were keeping it hot.

"Well," he said without preamble, sitting down to baked beans, tomatoes and tinned sausages, "it has begun."

"Did you bring the vanadium?"

"Actually, it wasn't ready, so I didn't have to pretend. I shall have to make another trip for it. If I can get a take-off without a lot of people hanging round, I will chance trying to smuggle you out. He might not miss you. Perhaps I could say you had stowed away somehow and escaped."

He shovelled beans uneasily.

"The trouble is, I shall have to come back without you, and then I must have an explanation. I doubt if he will believe that people can hide in helicopters. Perhaps under a rug or something? What about the trim? He is not a pilot, but he understands most things."

He turned to the old negro, who stood by the table, smiling, listening, mothering him to second helpings.

"The wire wasn't ready, Pinkie. I shall have to fetch it next time."

"Ought we to talk?"

"Pinkie doesn't mind," he said, pretending to dig him in the ribs with a fork. "Do you, Pinkie? All the tar-baby wants is to make vibrator units and fill us with beans — isn't it, you old Othello?"

He was given another spoonful.

"What has begun?" asked Nicky.

They were simmering to tell him about the new ally, but it would be better by keeping.

"Operation Overlord would be a good name for it, if it hadn't been used. Call it Operation Masterpiece if you like. We are at D-Day minus ten. It is in the papers. Look."

He tossed them a creased copy of the *Mirror*, with its pictures of girls in bathing dresses standing on tiptoe, hauling ropes in yachts to lengthen their legs and lift their bosoms. Its headlines were two inches high and said, THE MASTER?

"I thought he had to keep wireless silence?"

"Well, of course. But that doesn't prevent him posting letters. I take a mail-bag full every week, mostly the football coupons for the crew."

"It says," said Nicky, reading it out, "that a new weapon has been added to the horrors of modern warfare, with which the very roots of civilization and the hearthstone of the British home are being threatened. And on page six — turn to page six — there is another headline called A GRISLY HOAX? And Cassandra has got half a page saying it is because President Eisenhower plays golf, and the leading article says Sir Anthony Eden ought to retire, and — wait a bit — in the small print it explains that an unidentified scientist operating from some unknown hide-out threatens a supersonic blackout on August the tenth unless his demands are met. Why supersonic?"

"They have to say something."

"What. . . ."

"By the way," said Mr. Frinton, pausing with a sausage half way to his mouth, "I wonder if I could get you into a couple of mailbags? They are not very big."

Knowing what they now did about the co-operation of Mr. Blenkinsop, they were less interested in escape than they had been.

"What do people say?" asked Judy.

"Practically nothing. I was in a bus in Belfast when the papers came out, standing room only, and I hadn't time to buy one. I tried to read the headlines over a girl's shoulder. She was a typist, I think. Quite pretty. She didn't look at the front page at all, skipped page six upside down and began poring over Dorothy Poop. It was something about net stockings."

"Surely some people will be bothering?"

"In the evening I went to pubs. You can generally hear quite sensible talk in pubs. One man who looked like a churchwarden said 'it would interfere with the pools' and a docker said 'it was a plot by the Conservatives to interfere with the health scheme'. Nobody else said anything, not in that one. In the last one I went to, there was quite a conversation about it. The publican said, 'Will it turn the beer?' The barmaid said, 'Sure, we won't be able to see de reception for Frankie Sinatra on de Tay Vay'. And an old charlady in the corner asked, 'Will I get me chamber-pot back that me ould hellion av a sister-in-law was after linding to de Electric, or so she says?' "

"Is it meant to be propaganda?" asked Nicky. "Has it failed?"

"Not at all," said Mr. Frinton. "They are connecting it with things close to themselves, which is quite the best way of it not failing. I expect he will follow up with letters and advertisements for the next ten days, explaining a little more each time, but not saying where we are until he wants to start in earnest on D-Day. Then he will put down the bubble, and broadcast. Or will the bubble interfere with broadcasting? I posted a whole bagful of letters to newspapers in America and dozens of other countries. The mails will arrive in those countries at longer and longer intervals, and, when the letters are opened, the contents will reach the world's press at once. If I posted a letter to New York by airmail today, saying 'Bang' or something, the word Bang would reach the press four days hence, when the letter arrived. He could have posted a full plan of operations to Honolulu now, knowing that it wouldn't be opened in Honolulu before it had been put into action."

"But if they only worry about net stockings?"

"They have to begin worrying somewhere."

"Are you worrying?"

"Very much."

"We have," said Judy coyly, "a small thing to help unworry you. Something we have found out."

He was not much interested, except in the baked beans. He said, with his mouth full, "You don't say!"

"Guess what it is?"

"I haven't a notion."

"The Chinaman is on our side."

He put down his knife and fork and looked at them. There was no pleasure or anger or surprise or any other emotion in his face — only a steady look.

He said quietly, "Go on."

"We sort of investigated him."

"Yes."

"He thinks the Master ought to be stopped."

His hands were on either side of the plate, motionless, and there was a silence as if all three hearts had stopped.

He asked in a level tone, "Do you realize what a dangerous thing you have done?"

"He promised not to say anything."

"You had better tell me about it."

They told him in detail, just as we have seen it happen, while he stopped them every now and then to ask a question.

"Can you remember exactly what he said about being free to choose?"

"He said, 'It is a point of view.'"

"And he said, 'Mr. Frinton's heart is in the right place.' He said it like a sort of proverb."

"Neither of those are direct answers."

"But, sir," said Nicky, "he told us the absolute truth about everything, exactly the same as what you told us, only more. He wasn't trying to trick us like the Doctor."

"He is not such a fool."

"He didn't ask us to do anything."

He stared for a long time between his hands and said, "Well, you have told him anyway. What's to do now?"

They offered no suggestions.

"Listen, twins. I ought to tear you off a strip — but it wouldn't do any good. You don't know what you are doing. Please understand from now on that you are not to say anything to anybody. You are like a couple of monkeys playing round a power station, and if you pull the wrong handle it will be it. Just because a person tells you he won't repeat things, it doesn't mean that he won't — particularly in a place where brains can be open books — and because he says he wants to stop the Master it doesn't mean that he does. Do you really think that if he was against us he would tell you so? For all we know, he is pumping you for information. You really must be careful."

"He didn't exactly seem to be pumping. For one thing, he said he couldn't be any help."

"You have told him, at all events. It is no good living backwards. The question is, which way is forward now?"

His fingers drummed on the table.

He said thoughtfully, "Well, if he knows, he knows."

He stood up, pushing back the chair.

"Come along, we go and see him."

But when he was half way to the door he stopped.

"I don't want to go too much on the private side. Besides. . . ."

"I could fetch him," said Nicky.

They were both feeling very small.

"Do that thing."

CHAPTER TWENTY-THREE

A Choice of Tools

MR. BLENKINSOP was in a dragon gown for the evening, which they had not seen before. It was a gorgeous, snow-white robe of the Manchus, whiter than any laundry except a Chinese one could ever make it and it was at least fifty years old. The material was a thick, ribbed silk, much heavier than Shantung, embroidered in pastel shades and with real gold thread. There were nine gold filigree buttons. It had a high neck and wide sleeves. The dragons on it shimmered and swam with the delicacy of their colours, nothing brighter than the sides and lateral lines of a salmon or a rainbow trout, and the oriental gentleman inside it looked every inch heaven-born. Judy could have killed him to own the garment, which must have been worth three hundred pounds.

He was in an urbane humour, not necessarily a friendly one. He left it to Mr. Frinton to begin the conversation.

"Good evening."

"Good evening to you, sir."

"I hope Nicky didn't disturb you," said the Squadron-Leader. "It was kind of you to come."

"A pleasure."

"Do sit down."

Mr. Blenkinsop took the kitchen chair with the sweep of a cardinal sitting on his throne and looked at the other blandly.

"The children say that they have been telling you about me."

"That is so."

"It is not what I would have done myself."

"We are of a like opinion."

"But seeing that they have, I suppose we ought to talk it out?"

"It will be an agreeable conversation."

"More agreeable," said Mr. Frinton, "if you will lay off the Fu Manchu racket."

"As you say."

They were walking round each other's minds like dogs in a strange village, not knowing where trust should lie. They had lived together, for years longer than the twins had lived there, in an atmosphere to which tapped telephone wires or hidden microphones would have been child's play. In it, nobody knew what anybody else knew or meant to do, how much or how little. Reliability did not exist where treachery could be unintentional, by the transference of thought. Reticence was their only safeguard.

"They tell me you want to stop the Master."

"Yes."

"Why?"

No bid.

"It would help me if you could give a reason," said

Mr. Frinton. "After what has been said, we have to be frank."

"I should prefer not to be so."

"Very good."

"The fact remains that I desire to stop him."

"Yes. Another fact which remains is that you now know a lot about me, but I know very little about you. Are you suggesting that we should co-operate?"

"It seems better than acting at cross purposes."

"Will you answer questions?"

"Your mind is more easily read than mine."

"I keep away from the private side as much as possible."

"You visit it."

"I try to think about neutral subjects."

"You understand very little about it."

"I see."

"On the other hand, Mr. Frinton, the same circumstances which compel you to be frank are operative with me. I will do my best to answer questions, if they are compatible with safety. I must. We are not the masters of the situation."

"Have you taken any steps about stopping him?"

"There are none which I can take."

"You told the children that my idea of shooting at him was hopeless."

"You know it yourself."

"Why?" asked the Squadron-Leader, going back as in Snakes and Ladders. "If you would tell me *why* you wanted to stop him, it would help me to believe you."

"If I told you why," said Mr. Blenkinsop calmly, "you would refuse to co-operate."

"Then it is a bad reason."

"If you consider that all reasons unacceptable to yourself are bad, yes. What is 'bad'? "

"I see."

Somehow, this seemed to cheer Mr. Frinton up.

"At least," he said, "you are definite about it. It seems to clear the air a little."

"I am glad you think so."

"We have separate reasons for doing the same thing, I take it, and we must not work at cross purposes, but according to you the thing is impossible. Where do we go from there?"

"It is not at all impossible."

"How?"

"Mr. Frinton, I am afraid you underestimated the intelligence of Dr. McTurk. No, let me call it his cunning."

"He seems to have overestimated his own."

"That is the danger for us all."

"What was so cunning about him?"

"He knew how to choose his tools, even if he did not know how to handle them."

"What tools?"

The Chinaman waved a courteous hand — the false finger nails were on again — in the direction of Nicky.

"I refuse," said Mr. Frinton, for the third or fourth time, "to use the child as a cat's-paw."

"There is nobody else to use."

"It is impossible."

"Then the project is impossible."

"Quite apart from moral considerations, it is a wild idea on the . . . on the practical side. Can you see a boy of twelve pulling it off?"

"Children are more efficient than you think."

"But he has never fired a pistol. Have you? Anybody who hits anything at ten feet with a hand arm is practically a Colonel Cody. Or are you suggesting that a schoolboy is going to have the nerve to walk up to the Master while his back is turned and shoot him at close quarters, when squads of anarchists generally fail to kill archdukes? If he used my revolver he would be pottering about for half a minute trying to pull the trigger with both hands, and it would go off in the air, or shoot himself, or he would have forgotten the safety catch . . . Besides, what about his nerve? Children don't do these things."

"Your ideas about childhood do you credit, Mr. Frinton."

"Even if he is the only person whose intentions can't be read in advance, his actions themselves would give the necessary warning. How do we know that the Master is going to keep his back conveniently turned for half a minute while he goes through the drill, even if he has the nerve to want to, and what happens if he turns round?"

"Dr. McTurk had no plans about pistols."

The Squadron-Leader was not listening.

"You wouldn't do it, would you, Nicky? Be practical

and face it. It is like asking somebody to play tennis who has never seen a racquet."

"If you tell me to," said the hero-worshipper slowly and bravely and knowing what it meant, "I will try."

"Bah!"

Mr. Blenkinsop asked patiently, "Have you finished with firearms?"

"Well?"

"The Doctor was considering poison."

"Poison him yourself."

"Anything either of us does within his ambit is within his consciousness. Master Nicholas is the only avenue."

"You can't poison people."

"Is that a statement of fact?"

"We are not Borgias."

"It seems to me that the civilization of our own century is a good deal worse than that of the Renaissance — but do not let us embark on a discussion of history. Many people have been, are and will be poisoned. Indeed, I understand that the influential gangsters of the last war chose prussic acid for themselves, after considerable research, of their own accord."

"The wrong person always drinks it."

"Nobody drinks the Master's whisky."

"Where are you to get it, anyway?"

"After the Doctor was taken from us, since I had been following his line of thought, I did have the curiosity to glance along the shelves of his surgery. Unfortunately, the same idea must have occurred to the Master. There is nothing left stronger than indigestion tablets."

"You see."

"There is the helicopter."

"I should need a prescription or something. And there is the poison book to sign."

"I am a doctor."

"I will not go shopping for cyanide, to make a child do something because I want to do it myself. We don't even know that Nicky wants to. Do you?"

"Not much."

"He is not involved in this like us. The situation is not for children. He does not understand it. It is not fair."

"Fair?" sighed Mr. Blenkinsop.

"Besides, we do not know how long it will be before the Master reaches the boy's mind like ours."

"An additional reason for haste."

"What it boils down to is that you have wormed yourself into the confidence of these children and myself to get a poison which you can't get without me and to have it administered, which you can't do without them."

"That is so."

Judy said, "There is one other person with a free mind, apart from Nicky."

The Chinaman looked at her at once.

"He will not do it," he said.

CHAPTER TWENTY-FOUR

Pinkie

NEXT morning, hugging Jokey in bed, which was strictly forbidden at home, Judy said, "When it actually comes to murdering people, it's different."

"Yes."

"Like jumping off the diving board instead of standing on it."

"Yes."

"Would you, Nicky?"

He thought for a long time, then said, "No."

He added, to explain, "I should make a muck of it. Besides, you can't."

"Mr. Frinton was going to."

"Yes."

"I suppose it's easier to kill people when they are trying to kill you."

"It might be fun."

"Nicky!"

"Yes, in aerial combat or something. But not with poison and if he isn't. And too, I'm afraid."

"After all, he did murder Dr. McTurk."

"Yes."

"Which makes it more frightening."

"Yes."

"Things are different when they are real."

"Judy, it's more that you can't do it than being scared of him. It's more being scared of it."

"You *said* you would."

He answered after a time, maturely and painfully, 'How can people tell what they would do if they had to?"

"Why won't Pinkie do it? How does Mr. Blenkinsop know he wouldn't?"

"Nobody said."

"Has anybody asked him?"

"Judy, can you stop making questions? Where are our overalls?"

"Mr. Frinton forgot them."

"I mean the ones here, for you to mend."

She was a good girl and knew that he was in trouble. She said meekly, "I will ask Pinkie if he has seen them."

"Why can't we ask Pinkie ourselves? To kill him, I mean."

"Mr. Frinton was furious when we asked the China-man."

"He was not."

"He was, inside."

"Well, we could ask *him* to ask Pinkie. We could go together."

"If you murder somebody," mentioned Judy, "are they gone for ever? It would be pretty sickening meeting them in heaven."

"Oh, shut up. You don't understand a thing about it. Besides, you would be in hell."

"Will Jokey go to hell?"

"How am I to know? You are the one who knows everything."

"I'm not."

"You are."

"I'm not. And you do too."

"*Tu quoque.*"

"What's that?"

"Its the same as extemporary, ha, ha!"

After this victory, it was a fairly cheerful boy who set out with his sister to persuade Mr. Frinton to persuade the negro to murder the Master.

"Well, we might try," said the Squadron-Leader. "But if the Chinaman says he won't, he won't."

"Why?"

"Mr. Blenkinsop is cleverer than I am. He has probably tried him already."

"I don't see," said Nicky, "why there is such a fuss about giving the poison. I mean actually giving it. Personally, I think it is foul, but surely it's easy to give? He has to eat and drink, and you just put it in. You wouldn't even have to tell Pinkie what you had done. You'd put it into something he was taking there."

"But Pinkie doesn't cook for the private side. They look after themselves."

"Well, why can't Mr. Blenkinsop put it into something and forget about it?"

"Because everything that goes on behind the black door is under the Master's nose — his mind, rather."

"Anyway," said Judy practically, "we haven't got any."

"Even then," said the dogged Nicky, "let him put the stuff into something outside the door and then take the thing in and leave it about."

"Into what?"

"Oh, a cake or a whisky bottle or something."

"He would notice it being brought in. Nothing goes through the door without being checked in his mind, like a customs shed. You know, one of the troubles with you is that you are forgetting the Master. I can't think how you do, Nicky, with your afternoon lessons."

"I never forget him," said the boy sombrely, "and I know he is always a jump ahead."

"Realize it."

"Nicky says . . ."

"Listen, Judy, let me finish. What you have got to realize is that you are not in an interesting problem. You are in deadly danger. Has it properly dawned on you that he is more than thirteen times older than you are? Don't you see that everything we are saying at this moment has probably been foreseen? Even when we are out of sight or hearing, we are thinking the thoughts he was expecting us to think, perhaps before the Crimean War. What is so desperate about the situation is that now, but now, while we three go to see Pinkie, we are probably doing exactly what he expects us to do."

No, they had not thought of this. They did so, in a chilling silence.

"Never mind. The thing about life is to take it as it comes. We can't do better than our best. Let's get alongside this Pinkie job."

As they went down in the lift, he quoted to brighten them, "Its being so cheerful as keeps me going."

They found the negro making jam puffs for Jokey, who stood beside him in adoration, looking upwards like a sightseer admiring St. Peter's, Rome. When he put the jam in, she wagged her tail three or four times, in verification.

"Cupboard love!" said Judy disgustedly.

Jokey wagged twice more in an absent way, saying, "Yes, yes, another time."

It turned out that one of Mr. Frinton's many principles was not to use people unless they knew what they were doing. He would no more have asked Pinkie to do something unconsciously than he would take advantage of Nicky. This meant that he had to accept the risk of explaining what they wanted. But he had hardly started the recitation when he was stopped.

The blackamoor, smiling kindly and mysteriously, produced a cheap and battered wallet from the back pocket of his jeans and opened it with reverent fingers. It was evidently a valued article. Inside, there were his discharge papers from the 1914 war, saying that he had been a good soldier, a medal of the Rose of Lima, a recipe for making *boeuf à la mode*, a faded photograph of a piccaninny playing baseball, an advertisement for watchmaker's tools, and a much folded cutting from a newspaper. He put the last on the table in front of them, holding it carefully in his doughy fingers.

When some negroes smile, their mouths split open like a surgical cut, puffy at the edges. Pinkie's thick lips were beautifully moulded at the labial line, like the serene mouth of Rameses.

The newspaper picture was a photograph of Ghandi.

CHAPTER TWENTY-FIVE

The Eye of Balor

"I will chance it," said Mr. Frinton, "and try to get you out under the mailbags. Fortunately there is a heavy mail for the newspapers."

"If the Master is going to do something to the outside world, we might be better in."

"You will be better out of the way."

Nicky said, "I will try to give him something if you like."

"Rubbish."

They thought of home and the park with the ponies in it and the lake with its rotunda, where they used to have picnics before it had to be turned into a tea-house for the trippers. In the lake, there were pike, perch and tench — the latter of record size and perfectly uncatchable. They also thought, for once, of their parents, and their hearts melted. It would be like going home for the holidays!

"But we must take Jokey."

"Oh, Lord!"

"Judy can hold her mouth shut under her arm."

"One thing," said Mr. Frinton, accepting the

inevitable. "If the Master is having a walk, Judy must keep out of the way. She is the weakest one for being read. If we meet him, scram. You can't take any luggage, by the way."

"We haven't got any, except for these foul night-shirts."

The Master used to enjoy one daily walk, round the inside and on the crown of the islet, perhaps for exercise. He went at different times each day — according to Mr. Frinton, because it kept people alert or uncertain, if they didn't know when he would pass. Perhaps scared people do work better: at least Napoleon thought they did.

They were loading the helicopter, waiting for an opportunity to slip on board it — Mr. Frinton intended to make an opportunity, if necessary, by sending the engineers on errands — when a hush among the helpers made them turn.

He was coming, leaning on the Chinaman's arm.

The Master always went slowly, like something unimaginably old and automatic. He moved on his thighs and heels, not on his calves and toes. He did not give an impression of weak hams or of trembling fragility, though he must have been very fragile. It was more an impression of infinite experience — accustomedness. His fingers on Mr. Blenkinsop's sleeve had had so much practice at being fingers that they seemed to live a life of their own, independently, running about like mice on their private errands. The whole of him was withdrawn from its parts. Old ladies who are being photographed for the newspapers on their hundredth birthday, propped on their pillows, sometimes have these independent hands. And deaf people are sometimes withdrawn, in the same way. They sit, in the roar of the radio perhaps, with that strange look of being somewhere else — until suddenly they startle us by doing something unconnected with the music, like blowing their noses at the wrong moment.

He was in a plaid shawl — for some mysterious reason it was the grey Balmoral tartan.

But it was the eyes. Their lids were drawn down at the outer corners, hooding them in the calm, yellowish, distant, cellular, reserved antiquity of the vellum death mask — a mask which lived its life inside.

The Irish had a god once, called Balor. He only had one eye, but it was deadly. Its lid drooped over it. When his soldiers wanted to win a battle, they took their king to the front rank of the army, and hoisted up the eyelid, slaughtering all he looked upon.

As he came, the engineers fell silent. They withdrew for him to the sides of the hangar, like courtiers making a path for the King to come. Judy, who had begun to scuttle the moment he was sighted, flattened herself against the wall of the corridor to let him pass. He fixed her with that eye of lightning as she fled — fixed her silently, absently, without a sign of recognition. He stood beside the helicopter in a muse of prehistoric patience, while Mr. Blenkinsop, waving his free hand, motioned to everybody to go on.

Nicky thought, That's done it. Will he stay? And, as Judy vanished, two ideas came into his mind in a

blurred picture. They did not seem to be connected.
One was, did the Chinaman bring Him to prevent us
escaping? The other was, Is Pinkie a vegetarian?

He looked helplessly at Mr. Frinton, hoping for a
lead. But the Squadron-Leader was busy in the cockpit, his faculties concentrated on making his brain a
blank. He could give no help.

The work went forward.

Shall I go and look for Judy, thought Nicky?
Where will she have hidden? If he moves off, presumably she will come back. We must both be in the same
place. The worst thing is if two people start looking for
each other, because then neither of them knows where
the other one is. Best to stay here. She will know
where I am anyway. What is he thinking about?
Why doesn't he go?

But he didn't go.

The mail bags were stowed, the crane run over and
the hangar doors swung in. Lowered handily to the
summer ocean, the helicopter floated like a ping-pong
ball while its rotors were being fitted. Mr. Frinton,
keeping his head bent over maps and compass bearings
and controls, busied himself with anything that was
handy — with the trim, with the instrument panel,
with the cockpit drill for taking off. He made no sign,
nor even looked towards Nicky.

The shattering roar of the engine lifted all the birds
of Rockall.

As the helicopter grew small in the distance, buzzing
like a cockchafer or an angry hornet, the Master turned
to the boy. With effort, like somebody with a stiff back

bending to pick up a pin, he managed to say something without the help of whisky. It came out with creaking, ill-fitted tongue, like that of the monster made by Frankenstein.

He said, "Good day to you."

Nicky found Judy sitting on the floor of their bedroom, as white as lard, holding Jokey tightly by the collar.

"Ju!"

"Has he gone?"

"Mr. Frinton has gone."

"Did you hear Him?"

"No, what?"

"What He told me."

"Did he say something to you?"

"He said that Mr. Blenkinsop had brought Him to stop us going, and He was sorry we would have to stay a little longer, and it was no good approaching Pinkie because he is a believer in non-violence, and Mr. Blenkinsop had kindly told Him about that too, and anyway to look at Pinkie at dinner-time because whatever he serves other people he doesn't even eat meat himself, and . . ."

"What else did he say?"

She looked bewildered.

"Did he tell you anything else?"

"No — I don't think so."

She added defiantly, "No, nothing at all."

CHAPTER TWENTY-SIX

Evening Occupations

THE night before Mr. Frinton was due to return was breezy, so everybody listened to the weather forecast before they went to bed. While the wind streamed outside, flattening the breakers, the people of the island settled down to their evening occupations.

The twins lay flat on the floor in their hospital bedroom, reading a book between them which they had discovered in the men's library. Occasionally they pushed Jokey off, who, being no scholar, wanted to sit on it. It was a copy of the *Yachtsman's Annual* for 1949-50, and it had a long article called "Westabout to Rockall".

"Jeepers," said Nicky, "this is more up to date than 1896."

"But we are more up to date than it."

After a bit they began to fidget impatiently, ruffling the pages.

"Where *is* the Rockall part? What does *westabout* mean anyway?"

"Sailors say it, I expect. Like Westward Ho!"

"Do they say that? I thought it was golf?"

After searching for ages among the twenty-two pages, baffled by staysail, main, mizzen and jackyard topsail, they found half a page about the island itself.

"Here it is!"

"Look, they found 13 Guillemots, 15 Gannets, 50-70 Kittiwakes, 2 Herring Gulls, 2 Lesser Black-backs and 1 Great Black-back!"

"Tomorrow," said Judy importantly, "I shall count every single bird I see."

"One thing," said her brother in a pleased voice, "they didn't manage to land."

The engineers of the island, humble property men or extras in the drama of Rockall, had begun on their usual tasks. Those on duty still glanced at their slumbering or darting indicator-needles, wiping their hands on rags, while the off-duty watch meddled patiently with their glued feathers and bottled ships. The bottle-man was inserting a pinnace in the neck of his bottle, to make it a rarity — as this skill, or the addition of a miniature lighthouse, added to the value. The man of feathers had decided on a friendly inscription in the middle of the lid, and was spelling out CEAD MILE FAILTE on a scroll, with white plumage from Herring Gulls. He had left out the second L, which would be a disagreeable surprise for him when he noticed it.

Pinkie was about to take a shower in the wash-house. A huge, black-skinned Umslopagaas, his naked muscles gleaming like satin and sliding like pistons in spite of the frosty hair which crowned him, he stood with his arms apart, one hand on each wall of the shower, and looked down. There was a porcelain trough at the foot of the shower, about twelve inches deep, with a plug which could be fitted to make a shallow bath. In this steep and white-glazed basin, there was a spider with long legs and a small body. It could not climb out.

Pinkie, who had turned off the water the moment he saw the creature, stood with his weight on one leg, considering it. He was afraid to pick it up.

After a bit, he went to the wash-basins and fetched a nail-brush. He held this under the spider, which withdrew. He fetched a second brush and managed to lift it unharmed between the two of them, carrying it tenderly to the door of the bunk house, where he set it free.

Back in the wash-room, with the water once more hissing on the ebony shoulders, he stood like a statue in a Versailles cataract or the figure of Neptune in a Roman fountain. The steam hid him. He thought, A spider on Rockall? How did it get here? Perhaps it came with a cargo on the trawler. And he also thought — for he knew much more than people suspected: The first living being on Krakatoa after the eruption was a spider.

Mr. Blenkinsop was in his own room, meditating in one of his evening gowns, his hands folded in the sleeves.

It was true that he could have given more *chinoiserie* to the children. The walls of the room were lined with built-in cupboards, with plain doors which showed nothing, but which, if you opened them, displayed his collections of sword-furniture like tsubas or fuchis and cloisonné enamels and superb examples of satsuma — some crackled like the skull of the Master, some powdered with gold dust, some covered with a million distinct butterflies. From the lids of the faience there sprouted porcelain toadstools and gilded lions, snarling with their paws on lattice-work spheres. There were ivory figurines of fanciful coolies, half man half tortoise, hopping on one leg because they had stood on a toad perhaps — carved there, on the sole of the foot — and bronzes and alloys and gongs and miniature earthenware tea-sets galore, hidden by the cupboard doors. The Chinaman's taste tended towards the splendour of Japan. In the room itself, there were only two ornaments. One was an intricate picture of peacocks by Ganku, a positive Niagara of gorgeous feathers in infinite, delicate detail. The other was a lacquer shrine of Tsunayoshi, so intricately moulded and inlaid and appliquéd and champlevéd and repoussé, with so many lacquers of gold and black and vermilion, so tiered and terraced and pigeon-holed and pillared with niches, so overwhelmed with inset metals and glistening surfaces and sharkskin textures and sumptuous, scaly dragon-tails, that it was like an explosion of little doors, all open, and it seemed to glow with its own light.

In front of this, with his back to it, Mr. Blenkinsop sat on a plain mat with his eyes closed, thinking as little as possible.

The reason why he wanted to get rid of the Master was a simple one, and the reason why he did not want to bother Mr. Frinton by mentioning it was simple too. Like Totty McTurk, he desired to be the ruler of the world himself. But there was this difference between their attitudes. Totty had wanted power, which Mr. Blenkinsop did not want. It was not that he desired to rule, but to stop being ruled. Once the Master had united the nations, it seemed to him that the unifier would be redundant. It would be simpler to administer matters on his own account.

One of Mr. Blenkinsop's laws was simplicity. It was more efficient to tell as much truth as possible. He really did intend to get rid of the Master when the latter's work was perfected — he could apply it himself without help, from what he knew already — and to get rid of Mr. Frinton too, and anybody else if necessary, that is to say, if they turned nasty. Anything for a quiet life. Meanwhile, honesty was the best policy. The fewer lies he told, the less he had to remember them.

For the time being, the boy was needed on the premises.

In his own boudoir, the focus of treasons, stratagems and spoils, the Master sat by his radiogram listening to Bach. With an infinitely small part of his mind, he was playing solitaire. The cyanosed hands capered steadily about the board, clicking the marbles into place. As it was impossible for him not to get the game out, it was in fact a manual occupation, like knitting.

CHAPTER TWENTY-SEVEN

News Review

THE helicopter came buzzing into the level light of evening, blazing like a diamond grasshopper in the deep sky, as it breasted the dazzle of sun and sea. The twins were there to meet it.

"Mr. Frinton, it was the Chinaman who brought Him, to stop us getting away!"

He was not surprised.

"Well," he said cheerfully. "We ought to have thought of that."

"Why?"

"If Mr. Blenkinsop wanted to use Nicky, naturally he would not want him to go away."

"And he told the Master how we tried to persuade Pinkie!"

"Did he, indeed?"

"He is not on our side at all."

"You never know."

"How can he be, if he sneaks?"

"Perhaps we had better ask.

"Look," added the Squadron-Leader, "I must get on with stowing the coffee-grinder. I'll come and talk to Mr. Blenkinsop when I've finished. Here, take these papers with you, and read them in the kitchen till I'm ready. Tell Pinkie to get the dinner. You'll see that things have begun to hum."

He gave them the bundle of newsprint, and turned on his heel to attend the helicopter.

There was a picture on the cover of *Time* by Artzy-basheff, shewing an imaginary portrait of the Master made up from blued pistons, violet dials and various other metal parts in the manner of a calculating machine. One hand, with tubular fingers articulated by screws like a spanner, pointed to an ultimatum on a piece of coloured paper — arsenical green. Quite a proportion of the letterpress inside was devoted to the affairs of Rockall, though the island was not mentioned by name, as the Master had not yet said where he was. Under THE NATION, in a leading article, the editors had started off with, " 'Time is, Time was and Time shall be no more,' said the brazen head to monkish philosopher Bacon. This week Time threatened to fulfil the prophecy. U.S. policymakers . . ." Under THE PRESIDENCY, the twins learned that "By week's end President Eisenhower was saying: 'I don't rule out the possibility.' " In PEOPLE, there was the picture of a senator — who looked like a shifty gorilla trying to read a depilatory advertisement upside down — and the caption was *Sharps on Harps*. It said, "Investigator McGinty, currently addressing vibraharpist convention at Manhattan's Biltmore Hotel, revealed that insofar as Russian agents . . ." But enough of the senator. Or too much. SCIENCE was devoted to the

main article. This said, "Frosty-pating Sir Anthony
Eden warned scientists last week in Britain's House of
Commons that worrisome messages (*see* NATION)
published lately in the world's press need be no hoax.
Professor Hopkins, interviewed by Timeresearcher
Kathryn Danuta Hamburger, stated . . ." The aged
physicist's statement was about morals, not about
mathematics, and the Timeresearcher had been forced
to go further afield or fare worse. She had put
together an efficient pastiche about radar defences in
Alaska.

Life was barking up the wrong tree. In the absence
of definite information about the Master, it had
guessed that he might be inhabiting a space station
somewhere near the moon. The middle pages, superbly
illustrated in dramatic colours, showed a lot of craters,
twin stars, aurora borealis effects and men in rubber
suits blowing themselves hither and thither with com-
pressed air, regardless of the fact that there was no air
to blow against.

Even the *New Yorker* had sent their man Stanley to
interview a manufacturer of electronic equipment —
aged ninety-nine, as an additional attraction — who
had returned with a collection of notes about sky-
scrapers written on an envelope.

The American reaction was alert, and therefore
more intelligent than the English one. It lacked the
phlegm of the British, which sometimes gets called
stupidity by the people whom it irritates, but it had
the advantage of being alive and speculative and willing
to worry about things, even if it worried wrong.

There were various other papers bundled with the ones from the United States.

Punch had a joke in Charivari; the *New Statesman and Nation* was whining about unfairness to minorities, presumably represented by the Master (of whom there was only one); and even the reviewers of *The Times Literary Supplement*, pausing for a moment in their tireless anonymous vendetta, had cast a supercilious eye on nuclear physics.

There was no Russian comment. The Americans suspected that *Pravda* was holding its hand, pending the claim to have invented whatever it was that the Master had invented.

All this was above the children's heads. They were not impressed by it — though it did throw some light on the way the crisis was brewing. Bad situations often do begin with farces, and perhaps because of them. The French Revolution was preceded by a discussion of the advantages of cake as an alternative to bread — if bread should prove to be too expensive — and an English lord during the Irish famines once came out rather strongly in favour of issuing curry powder. In the midst of life we are in death.

Mr. Frinton came to the kitchen, rubbing his hands.

"What's for dinner?"

He was in a good humour because he was in danger — as they all were — and this had freed his sense of comradeship, rather as the blitz did in 1940.

Nicky said, "We are sick of being dressed up as pantomime fairies. Would you please ask somebody to look for our overalls, as Judy says she might be able to mend them?"

"I never did."

"You. . . ."

He was absolutely flabbergasted by the sheer, feminine, immoral untruthfulness of it.

"Besides, there is no thread."

"Yes, there is thread. I saw some in the . . . in the. . . ."

"Well, where?"

"What about the man who rigs the ships in bottles? He's got thread."

"It's not the right kind. Besides, he's using it."

"Why do you always say 'besides'? Everything is besides everything is besides everything is besides . . ."

"Boo."

He said with concentrated loathing, "You are a *slop*."

Mr. Frinton said, "Bite him, Jokey."

He turned despairingly on the newest persecutor, betrayed even by his own sex.

"But she *said* . . ."

"I didn't.'

He threw the newspapers on the floor.

"How do you know you didn't say what you don't know that I was going to say you did?"

"Like a biscuit tin," said Judy complacently.

"*What?*"

"On biscuit tins there are pictures of boys holding biscuit tins with pictures of boys holding biscuit tins on them and so on ad lib."

"Ex temporary too, I suppose."

"Yes, ad lib, and ex temp. and too crokey to you."
He clenched his fist.

"Meanwhile," said Mr. Frinton, "it is tinned
spaghetti for dinner. And, oh Pinkie, before I forgot,
there's a parcel of vanadium for you in the hangar."

CHAPTER TWENTY-EIGHT

Poison

THEY were having a coffee party in Mr. Frinton's sparely furnished cabin. Good men and true have theories about tea, coffee and sometimes even cocoa. They are more sincere theories than the pretentious poses about vintage wine which far too many people invent. Mr. Frinton did not care whether he was drinking Chateau What's-its-name, and would gaily have shaken up a bottle of crusted port, but he did devote the attention of an old maid to the making of hot drinks. His theory about coffee was that it must not on any account be allowed to come in contact with metal.

This theory, to be valid, had to overlook the fact that the grains had been ground by machinery and sold in a tin.

He warmed the pot, measured the coffee and sugar into it with a wooden spoon from a plastic container, poured in the boiling water and stirred.

After eighty seconds, measured by the clock, he strained the liquid into their cups through a metal strainer — averting his mind from this — and, what with one thing and another, it was excellent.

To the surprise of the twins, he shewed no animosity against Mr. Blenkinsop about his trick in the hangar.

The latter, who was in an evening robe, had brought with him four of his best satsuma cups to speed the merriment, and he sipped from one of them smilingly, looking like a Buddha in a monastery or a cat who had swallowed the goldfish. He even teased Mr. Frinton, and the latter teased him. They had both had a good deal of education from the Master — much more than Nicky had had — and they were more accustomed to the dreadful diplomacy of Rockall.

The crisis had stimulated them.

When they had finished teasing, they came to business.

"Why did you have to tell him about Pinkie?"

Mr. Blenkinsop spread out one deprecating, long-nailed hand.

"One has to say something."

"How much did you tell?"

"Nothing damaging, I promise you. It seemed wiser to offer as much information as possible — as you will be the first to recognize, my dear chap. How do you put it? To add verisimilitude to an unconvincing narrative."

"What exactly?"

"Naturally I mentioned that you had been approaching Pinkie to do away with him."

"It seems a little unfair?"

"Not at all. Master Nicholas — not Pinkie — is the one who is going to be useful to us, so there could be no danger to anybody except the negro."

"Leaving out the risk to Pinkie," said Mr. Frinton, beginning to look fierce, "what about me?"

"No danger in the world. The Master cannot fly a helicopter."

"I see."

"Mr. Frinton," said the Chinaman, turning to the twins, "is such a fire-brand! So warm-hearted! His generous nature betrays him into impulse, which — hum — 'o'erleaps itself and falls on the other'."

"I don't see," said Nicky, "why he should be particularly pleased if you tell the Master that he wants to kill him."

"But he does want to."

"If he is warned. . . ."

"Mr. Blenkinsop means that the Master probably knows already," said the Squadron-Leader, his look of exhaustion beginning to come back. "It is true."

"Also, of course, nobody on the island is in danger until he becomes useless."

"You mean that so long as he needs his helicopter, I shall be kept in being."

"Just so. And Pinkie will be kept until he has finished the vibrator unit.

"The risk," continued Mr. Blenkinsop, explaining, "was scarcely more than the existing one."

"I see."

After a bit, Mr. Frinton asked, "What about your own uselessness?"

"In that event," said Mr. Blenkinsop, faithful to the labour-saving principle of truth, "I shall endeavour to replace him."

"What it boils down to is that you are using *us* to help *you* to become the Master?"

"In a nutshell."

"And in that event also," said the Squadron-Leader in a rage, "I may warn you that I shall make it my personal business to replace you."

"You will be welcome to try."

Mr. Frinton swallowed the violence which was rising in his gullet.

"Do you seriously think that we would kill one man to put up another?"

"First things first," said Mr. Blenkinsop reasonably. "Everything in due order. After Master Nicholas has killed the Master, you only have to kill me."

And he put down the coffee cup, to nurse a thin-skinned knuckle inside the other palm.

One of the best ways to disarm criticism is to accept it.

"Look," said Mr. Frinton, "the boy is out of this, once and for all."

"You have failed to bring the cyanide?"

"Of course I have not brought it."

"Never mind. The substance is used to plate the contact points of Pinkie's vibrator units with platinum. We have some here already. I remembered this after you had left."

"Are you sure that the Master will not have remembered it?"

"Not at all sure. However, nothing venture nothing win."

They looked at him, wondering whether it was possible to be so calm about being such a villain.

"In any case, the boy is not going to be used."

"Mr. Frinton, will you, as a personal favour to me — considering our long association — examine a few facts without prejudice?"

"No."

"The children," said Mr. Blenkinsop patiently, "have mentioned to me their moral objections to vivisection. You have been taught a little biology yourself. Do you seriously believe that the sufferings of a few unfortunate dogs were not outweighed by the discovery of a vaccine against rabies? Do you remember what Napoleon said when they blamed him for the murder of the Duke of Enghien? Do you honestly think that the destiny of the whole of civilization is less important than the welfare of one small boy?"

"As to your second question," said Mr. Frinton, who had not been an island pupil for nothing, glancing along at the shelf of history books and selecting the right one, "Napoleon said, 'What, that d'Enghien affair? Bah! What is one man, after all?' "

"Napoleon was an authority on casualties."

"I don't intend to be."

"My dear Squadron-Leader, you are one already. Were there no casualties in the Hitler war?"

"Many of my friends were killed — for what they believed in."

"And do you suppose that they were not often sent into battle by commanders who did not expect them to return?"

"They knew what they were doing and they were not children."

"On the contrary, many of them were scarcely six or seven years older than Master Nicholas is — few of them did know what they were doing — and I should like to have your views on their conscription for national service?"

"I don't intend to conscript Nicky."

Nicky said, "He sometimes asks me to pour out his whisky, if Mr. Blenkinsop isn't there. Or he holds out his hand for it."

"The boy is willing."

"But I am not."

"In that case, it seems to depend on the boy."

"Nicky, you must snap out of this Treasure Island stuff. You know very well you couldn't pull it off, and that it is murder, and that these things don't happen to children."

"Why not?"

"Because . . ."

"In effect," said Mr. Blenkinsop comfortably, "a great many children have been accomplished murderers. What about the Salem witch hunts? What about David and Goliath?"

Nicky asked, "Do you need much?"

"A toothful."

To everybody's surprise, Mr. Frinton gave in without another word.

"We can get some from Pinkie's shelves," he said, "without bothering him about it."

"When?"

"Now," said Mr. Blenkinsop firmly. "Every moment's delay is another moment in which things may go wrong. All this 'beating about the bush' has been dangerous as well as tedious in the extreme. You can take it to him this evening, as it is his Saturday for whisky."

Nicky's heart went into his boots.

"Now?"

"In twenty minutes."

Judy said, "Sorry, I must go to the loo. I think I am going to be sick."

"Don't open the bottle till you are ready," said Mr. Blenkinsop slowly. "Don't sniff it. Don't spill it. Don't hurry. First pour out the tumbler of whisky, then open the bottle and put it in. You had better keep your back turned, but don't be hasty or furtive. Just pretend to yourself that you are pouring out a dose of any ordinary medicine and that your back happens to be turned. Then put the tumbler in the hand which he is holding out. He will drain it automatically, without waiting to taste or smell."

Judy came back with the Master.

CHAPTER TWENTY-NINE

The Empty Robe

SHE had gone the lard-colour again. She stood against the wall, looking straight in front of her as if her eyes were out of focus. She had been to fetch him.

Nicky realized it at once, without resentment or shock, remembering her meeting in the hangar and understanding that she could not help herself in what she did. She had been willed in that one glance to wait for the moment of treachery, and to report it.

Her mind was the Master's, and it knew their plans.

Between the trigger and the stricken deer, between the torpedo and the impact, between the sentence and the execution, between the action and the realization, there comes a pause. People who are listening hard hold their breath. The heart stays beatless, the lung half expanded, the blood poised below the ear lobe. No hand stirs, no foot falls. Time halts its traffic. Space stands still. Doom says: Now.

The two men stood to their feet. Nicky copied them, feeling groggy. The two, like Judy, were inside the eggshell of influence and had no will.

The Master came without haste, followed, even at

that distance from his quarters, by the frightfully inappropriate strains of the *Pirates of Penzance*. It would have been better if it had been a Funeral March. He had a bottle of whisky in one hand, to make himself conversible. The eye of Balor was perhaps a little brighter, and the whole body perhaps a little fuller, as if the veins had distended or the mind had taken a deeper breath of power. Once he was in the room, nobody else existed. His expression, so far as the marble face could have anything so fleeting, was one of suffering. Prometheus on his rock, after many centuries of eagles, might have borne his torments with the same remote patience.

He went up to Mr. Frinton and looked him deeply in the eyes. He said, with the thick tongue of an unaccustomed speaker, "Let me see. What would be most convenient?"

He turned to Mr. Blenkinsop, like somebody consulting other volumes in a reference library, and examined his eyes too.

Lastly he came to Nicky and for a long moment paused in inquiry, searching for the entrance — until, to the boy's swimming gaze, the two eyes merged into one, a blue diamond.

He went back to the Squadron-Leader.

"Mr. Frinton."

"Sir."

"You have been conversing about Napoleon."

"Yes, sir."

"Allow me to remind you of another aphorism thrown out by that great man. 'I know well,' he said, 'that nowadays it requires a rod of iron to rule men. It is necessary one should talk of liberty, equality, justice, and disinterestedness, and never grant any liberty whatever. I answer for it that they may be easily oppressed . . . without . . . really feeling any discontent.' "

"Yes, sir."

"Without feeling any discontent, Mr. Frinton."

"Yes."

"It is for their own good."

"Yes."

"Repeat it."

"It is for their own good."

"You are convinced that the welfare of humanity can best be served by me."

"I am convinced."

"In that case, let us resolve the situation in as few moves as possible. 'Set a thief to catch a thief.' "

"Yes, sir."

"You will prefer to constitute yourself a gaoler to this dangerous young man — whose liberty threatens the arrangements. You will take him and his sister to the hospital ward and there you will remain with them as a guard, till further orders. Nobody will leave the ward."

"I would prefer it."

"Thank you, Mr. Frinton. You may go."

They had opened the door, a mute procession of delinquents, when he called them back.

"Visit the negro on your way and tell him to bring your meals to you. While there, return his chemicals."

The Empty Robe

As the Squadron-Leader picked up the bottle of cyanide, the Master repeated with what might have been irony,

"Waste not, want not."

They went, and closed the door.

He turned to Mr. Blenkinsop.

In the now emptier room, under the shadeless light, to the background of a ticking clock, the two men stood together in silence.

A strange feature was that — before they left — Mr. Blenkinsop took off his gown and hung it carefully on one of the pegs beside Mr. Frinton's duffle coat. He did not want the beautiful embroidery to be destroyed as well.

CHAPTER THIRTY

Operation Masterpiece

WHEN the last vibrator-unit had been put together and all of them switched on, facing outwards from Rockall, one of the first results was that the lovely birds were killed. The Gannets floated with their wings open and their heads under water, dozens of white crosses with black wing-tips, gently rising and falling on the wave. Fish also came to the surface, belly-upwards, and in some patches made a carpet of silver, which undulated.

About thirty miles from the island, an airliner, caught in passage to Gandar on its great circle course, dived twenty thousand feet into the sea in one superb arc, and vanished in a fountain, like a distant iceberg, among a school of dead whales. The tail unit came up again because of trapped air and floated for a long time in company with the other monsters.

Fishing fleets between Iceland, Faroes, Hebrides and Malin Head were put out of action. They drifted, their crews desperately ill. Eight ships in the same sea area were upset according to how near they were to Rockall. All the passengers of a Greek vessel jumped overboard — but, strangely enough, were picked up again, hysterical, with no loss of life.

Messages by Atlantic cable ceased, local radio became confused, and an international pigeon race as far away as Manchester was disorganized, all the birds being lost.

People within a circle which passed more or less through Reykjavik, Edinburgh and Dublin complained of fearful headaches, palpitations, laryngitis and afflictions of the ear, nose and throat. The ones living in sea ports on the west of Scotland and Ireland, as well as in Iceland, were agonized by a ringing note which seemed to arch over them in the sky and to come from all directions at once. Some of them described it as bell-like, while others said it was like an air-raid siren. They disagreed as to whether it warbled or pierced — whether it was high or low — or whether it was like the note you get when you rub a wine-glass rim with your finger. In fact, it was a mixture of tones, and it did summon its decibels from space on frequencies both high and low, so that what you heard depended on how you were listening. Many were inaudible to man.

News services soon began to break down. Reporters who were near enough to hear the noise could not telephone descriptions of it, because the telephones were out of action, while the general collapse of machinery, and sickness among mechanics, stopped the printing of coastal papers.

Metal seemed to be damaged more than flesh was.

Rigid materials were spoilt more quickly than elastic ones, so that a living being lasted better than a piece of wood and a piece of wood better than a piece of iron.

The death rate went up, as in a smog, among very old people, very young people or the ones who were ill already.

Minor oddities were noticed. Milk soured as a matter of course, while a well-known brand of furniture polish turned everything green. People with metal fillings in their teeth were tortured with toothache, and several cases were reported of people who picked up distant broadcasts inside their own mouths. The bass singers in radio operas were heard as altos. Bees swarmed. Bats and snakes became active. Late chrysanthemums flowered early.

The effect on sick people was not always bad. Those with neuritis, tuberculosis and complaints of the liver got better. Convicts in prisons and lunatics in asylums tended to waves of violence — but lunatics at large, like the orators in Hyde Park, became composed and stopped addressing their audiences.

Boston is about 800 miles further from Rockall than Mocow is. The radius of the Master's ultimatum, which was to be widened by two hundred miles every day, would be well across Russia before it reached Chicago. Meanwhile, before the two great powers of the world could be reached by it at all, the greater part of Europe would be paralysed from Narvik to Naples to Gibraltar — as an example and a threat — while people would be dying from Glasgow to Cork.

The vibrators were housed on the cliff top in the open air, their sectors of influence overlapping off shore.

CHAPTER THIRTY-ONE

Foxed

NICKY said, "But you *can't* suddenly turn round and say the opposite."

So far as anybody could see, Mr. Frinton and Judy were as friendly to him as ever, as normal and as sensible. Only they were the opposite of themselves. They were pained by Nicky's stupidity, and did their best to enlighten or convince him.

"Nicky, do look at it in a grown-up way. Here we are in a world which has gone maverick, being governed by a lot of homicidal clots who could blow the whole concern to bits at any moment. Surely it is more sensible to have one wise man controlling operations than all these bolshevik jobs and Senator McCarthys? For one thing, don't you see that there can be no more wars? How can you have a war when there are no countries to have it against? The world will be like counties. Sussex doesn't go to war with Kent."

"I know. But . . ."

"It may mean that people get killed a little at first. It's a hateful thought, but it must be. It's Nature.

When gardeners want fruit and flowers, they have to kill snails and insects, however kind they are. You can't help it. Think of the good which will come of it, not the bad."

"Does good come out of bad?"

"Yes, in Nature."

Nicky said miserably, "I wish I had not been born in Nature at all."

"Well, you have been."

They were sitting on the iron beds, keeping half an eye on Jokey.

The latter, worn down by the hardships of island life, had gone psychic. She saw the ghosts of flies where no flies were and stood in front of their imaginary positions, pointing like a setter.

The prisoners had pencils and paper to amuse themselves, like children in a boring nursery on a wet day. With these they sometimes played dull games of Consequences or Noughts and Crosses — both freely described by Mr. Frinton as being The End. The rest of the time they argued.

"He will probably take over the existing machinery and direct it. It's surprising how the smallest alterations can make great changes. When they called themselves the South Saxons and the Men of Kent, the kingdoms could go to war. They only had to call themselves Sussex and Kent — counties — and it stopped. But they were the same places all the time. He won't have to alter the world, you know, Nicky. It could be almost the same, but better."

"I don't understand politics."

"It's no good criticizing for personal reasons."

"Why not?"

"Because Truth is above People. A thing is either right or not."

"Who said so?"

This put Mr. Frinton back on his heels, and rightly so, as it was the $64,000 question.

"What I mean is . . ."

Judy said, "Mr. Frinton always did explain that he believed in a — a unified world."

"He also explained that thing about evolution. Ants and things. I can't remember exactly what it was."

Nor could Mr. Frinton. It had been wiped from his mind.

"Judy, darling, listen. Ten seconds before you fetched the Master, you wanted to murder him. Ten seconds afterwards, he became the sort of White Hope of Christendom. Can't you see that something must have happened?"

"We were wrong," they said, in unison.

"Is it right to keep me here as a prisoner? Your own brother?"

"Yes, while you are being silly it is. You might go off and try to kill him."

"How could I?"

"It is not impossible," said Mr. Frinton. "You are a strong boy, and he is frail."

"I would," said Nicky desperately. "I would kill him if I could. He has wrecked you all, and stolen your minds, and foxed the people I love."

Nicky was in love. It was as much with his sister as with the Squadron-Leader.

Sometimes it is difficult to remember the purity and intensity of being young — when life is all excitement and ambition and confident anticipation of goodness and vivid love or dread. He really would have died for them. At least he felt that he would — felt he would like to have the chance to do so — and perhaps he might have done. There is no need to laugh at Wordsworth and his clouds of glory.

So it was a torment to watch them deadened in their minds, made mummers of or puppets, while their arguments beat his own and their warm hearts showed the numb side. It was desolating to be an outcast from their councils, a captive, a helpless spectator too, while everything they really stood for turned on itself with poison — a scorpion's suicide.

His reasons and pleas were helpless against theirs. He was in Coventry.

Perhaps this is what hurts young people most — to be cut off and left out.

He hated, he hated, he hated the Master. If, before — since he was not suggestible — he had sometimes felt a fear or dislike or even some of the contemptuous pity which the young feel for the old, he now felt the true emotion of blind rage. He truly longed to crush the infamy.

In the darkness, after lights-out, he wrote in large letters on one of the bits of paper — holding the pencil point at his finger-tip because he could not see.

He managed to push the message under the door

next morning after breakfast, on the pretence of playing with Jokey.

It said,

PINKIE PLEASE GET ME OUT OF HERE PLEASE.

CHAPTER THIRTY-TWO

Various Statistics

W<small>ITHOUT</small> Mr. Blenkinsop to help him, the Master had a task which would have been beyond other people. His staff had been cut down.

It was easy for Mr. Frinton to say that the Master was going to present an ultimatum and back it with the frequency mechanism. Anybody could present ultimatums. The difficulty was to get an answer and enforce it. The actual details and political problems of dealing with dozens of governments would have kept the secretariat of the United Nations busy for several years. But there was no time for that.

One of the problems was simply to get an answer. The vibrators blocked the use of radio. They would have to be switched off to pick an answer up. When they were switched off, they stopped giving a protective layer, so that the island became vulnerable to guided missiles or even aircraft. Nor could the fact that they had been switched off be hidden, because the global headache stopped at once and everybody knew.

When the puzzle of reply had been solved, there remained the question of whether it could be relied on.

Who was to give the answer? If congresses and senates and parliaments and presidiums were to vote on the subject, it would become one of those debates which go on for years — but, if President Eisenhower was taken as speaking for all, there was still no certainty that his word would be honoured by the masses. The Master remembered President Wilson.

Even if a word was given by the masses, it was not certain that it would be kept. The diplomacy of the Master's younger days — when it was possible that governments might keep their promises — had long been overset by the proceedings of Lenin and Hitler.

The mere number and different kinds of government which were involved had to be simplified. In a twenty-four-hour day it would have been impossible to deal with everybody from Liberia to Thailand.

The people of China, for instance, would take the destruction of Europe calmly — until their own cities began to be destroyed.

The vast number of these practical questions was added to by the hostile actions of some of the victims.

The Americans, although at first they were threatened least, were the quickest to react. The details of the programme were printed on the front pages of the newspapers as the calculated postal delivery came in. In this programme, the Master had explained what he intended to do and how, and where he was. This was a challenge to the ingenuity of an imaginative nation, so they had at once set on foot a series of countermeasures — which had to be foreseen and blocked.

Attack by aircraft or guided missiles or motor

vessels, on or under the surface, was found to be useless. It was seen at once that the means of getting
there must be natural. A mechanized world was back
again in the days of Drake, when a fire-ship driven by
the wind could be more successful than an atomic
submarine. But fire-ships were difficult to steer. No
crew could survive within 200 miles of Rockall and it
was not possible to set a course over that distance by
the wind. The wind seemed to be the clue. Technical
suggestions about poison gas or atomic fall-outs were
raised at once. A salvo of atomic shells exploded in the
sea to the west or south-west of the island, and two or
three hundred miles away from it, might be able to
shower it with radio-active dust carried by the wind.
Or perhaps a gas could be sent there in the same way.
But any gas or any fall-out laid down on a front broad
enough to cover variable winds, and concentrated
strongly enough to last over 200 miles, would certainly
go out of control and cut a swathe round the globe.

These attempts, which he had foreseen, prevented
him from lifting the curtain long enough to get an
answer.

The people of China might take the destruction of
Europe calmly. This was the point. The details of
answer and guarantee, by hostages or other means,
were unimportant compared with the central fact of
how the threat was made. It was plain that if everybody everywhere could instantly get the headache
himself, it would be easier to get things done.

The Master was aware of the quotation from Freud

once mentioned by Mr. Blenkinsop. A good surgeon cuts firm and deep, without faltering into snippets. The plain fact of the matter was that unless the ultimatum could be brought home everywhere at the same time, it was beyond one man to control it, because some people would be taking it seriously while others were not.

The range of interference had to be extended to include the whole world, for a few moments at any rate.

Unfortunately, the concentration needed for this would certainly kill several millions of people — the ones nearest to Rockall.

Great Britain, one of the most heavily populated places on the earth, was the nearest. Fortunately the corresponding areas to the north, west and south were empty ocean.

The population of Great Britain had lately been calculated at 50,535,000, while that of the whole world was 2,337,400,000 souls — if we adopt the Russian census for their people in 1900. To abolish the British would mean killing about one person in forty-eight. The Master doubted whether this was enough to solve the conflict of interests mentioned by Freud.

He sat at the chess table in the laboratory, working out the simple sums with a cheap atlas and a copy of Whittaker's Almanac. Seventy years ago, he might have been irritated by the lack of Dr. McTurk or some other secretary to do the job for him. Now, like a grandfather playing patiently with the baby's bricks, he clumsily manipulated, with forgetful fingers, a pencil and a sheet of paper.

During the Napoleonic wars — he remembered — the stalwarts of Nelson's navy had been expected to lose one in three before they struck their colours. The scholars of Eton — more privileged than naval tars — had in the present century paid for their privileges by accepting twice that rate of casualties. In the first world war, the Central powers had mobilized 22,850,000 people, of whom 3,386,200 had been killed before the powers collapsed. Call it one in seven.

Probably — he decided — it would be better to wipe out even more than the British.

It was an excellent idea, really, when you considered the findings of Malthus. According to Berle, the world's population, if unchecked, would increase by half between 1940 and 1965. Uneconomic.

Meanwhile, there were a thousand details to attend to, single-handed. The vibrators needed inspecting. It was time for the daily walk.

CHAPTER THIRTY-THREE

The Tempest

ONE of Pinkie's duties while they were locked up was to take Jokey for a stroll on the cliff top. When he came to fetch her that evening he produced his slate for messages, on which was written, MASTER WANTS KEY.

Mr. Frinton stood up, fished the key out of his pocket and handed it to the negro.

Pinkie nodded, held the door open for Jokey, jerked his head to Nicky, and followed the boy outside. He locked the door behind them.

It was as easy as that.

He went back to the kitchen without comment, as if he preferred to know nothing, leaving the two of them outside.

Nicky leaned against the wall for a moment with a thundering heart.

He took the key out of the keyhole and put it in his own pocket, pulling himself together. He thought to himself in a detached way, as if he were a stranger outside his body asking it questions, Am I afraid?

No, I am interested. This is peculiar. I know what I have to do and I realize that one of the people inside me could get into a panic if I let him, but if I take the steps which I have mapped out for myself this person will be blocked out or ignored or excluded or sort of censored, and the steps will take themselves — sort of. In any case, if I die, I die. All is Fate. Am I excited? No, I am keyed up. I am an efficient self-acting machine, and I must do my things in due order, first A, then B. Press button B.

Odd sayings passed through his head from time to time, like this one from the telephone boxes, as if the people inside him were calling each other's attention to them. One of them was the last line of his father's favourite song, which said, *Hustle Your Horse And Don't Say Die*. He found to his surprise and annoyance that he had repeated this line about fifty times. He was still repeating it, in tune. He made a conscious effort to hum *Rule Britannia* instead.

Mr. Frinton's old-fashioned revolver was in his cabin, in the usual drawer. It was loaded.

Nicky was used to firearms because of the gun-room at Gaunt's Godstone — which, incidentally, had a trophy from the first world war exactly like this one. He knew about safety catches and how to break the barrel to look inside for cartridges, which he did. But he had never fired one.

Hustle your horse and don't say die.

The best place to look would be on the Private Side. He went down in the lift, and there was the ebony door — somehow charged with power like the one

at 10 Downing Street — standing open. The antlers in
the hall had been pulled down and the laboratory
stood open — whose gleam and hum he saw for the
first time. There was nobody inside. There was a
presence in it, a consciousness, but no people. The
ancient boudoir or Baker Street smoking-room was
empty, its radiogram silent. Mr. Blenkinsop's bedroom, beyond one of the doors, glittered with the
deserted splendour of its lacquer shrine. The bathroom
and lavatory had — as Judy would have liked to know
— proper plumbing. Mr. Blenkinsop's false teeth —
a spare set — grinned in a tumbler of disinfectant on
one of the shelves. They were the basic symbols of a
skeleton, and all that was left of Mr. Blenkinsop.

He paused outside what must be the Master's bedroom, dreading to touch the handle. If he touched it,
it might fly or yawn open, perhaps inwards — which would
be worse — like a Jack-in-the-Box or Pandora's Box or
anything awful, and there would be what? He must not
imagine what. Hustle your horse and don't say die.

No. Rule Britannia.

The bedroom was empty. It was very plain — just
a camp bed made of iron and a peculiar sort of dumb
valet in mahogany, after the style of a dumb waiter.
When the Master was younger, gentlemen's bedrooms
often did have these contraptions — which looked like
complicated chairs fitted with shelves and coat-hangers
and boot-trees and even a wig-stand. There was a
button-hook on one shelf and a set of cut-throat razors
marked with the days of the week. The room smelt
faintly of bay rum.

Down the worn stair carpet, past the visiting card from Charles Darwin, along the tiled tunnel to the lift.

Just my luck, he thought, to have Jokey underfoot at this moment. Shall I shut her in one of the cabins? I had not thought this out. Yes, I will. No, I won't. It doesn't matter. I must go on being automatic and not stop to think about side-issues. Let her come with me, if she wants.

He could see into the engine room, where the men moved on their errands, not aware that they were watched.

Pinkie was in the kitchen, kneading dough. He did not look up.

Shining passages and shut doors.

The bunk-house was empty — its bottled ship completed, drying in a warm smell of glue.

The helicopter stood in the deserted hangar, secret and silent — a praying Mantis, a Pharaoh housed in his pyramid.

When Nicky opened the upper doors into the last dregs of daylight, he was nearly blown backwards.

He had been locked up for so long in artificial light without a window that he had forgotten about the weather.

Perhaps the vibrators had interfered with the atmosphere or with some other balance — for a tremendous storm was raging, in which lightning managed to combine itself with gale. The black sky — which Shakespeare might have expected to pour down stinking pitch upon the strong-based promontory — was full of mutinous winds and the dread-rattling thunder.

The waves were tearing along in serried ranks. They carried the spray, blown backwards from the breakers, trailing it behind them in osprey plumes which he could see through, like muslin. There were rainbows in it. The waves were dervishes doing a maniac dance of seventy-seven veils. The anemometer on the cliff top was a blur. The force-eight stream of air pressed the boy back against the rock.

He fought his way along the ledge to the summit.

He was rebellious Ariel, seeking a dreadful Prospero — in defence of Caliban — in the Tempest.

> *Every journey has an end*
> *When the worst affairs will mend.*
> *Dark is the dawn when day is nigh.*
> *Hustle your horse and don't say die.*

When Nicky found the Master, he was propped against the hurricane on his alpenstock, and the lightning zazzed.

He turned round laboriously, while the boy lifted the revolver — which yawed and wavered in the wind.

The Master came straight to the muzzle, leaning sideways to support himself, and there they stood on the slant, one pace away from each other.

The blue eyes came together as before, into one eye. The headlight grew until it filled the firmament, bearing down upon him like an advancing car to run him over. It began to spin like a catherine wheel. It was the universe, and it blazed, and he had to swallow or enter it.

He entered.

He lowered the revolver.

He said, "Yes."

He tossed the gun aside with a drowsy motion. He was inclined to sleep, with a good dullness, and give it way. The Webley skittered along the bare rock, spun round on its drum and vanished over the edge.

The Master had found the way to his mind.

CHAPTER THIRTY-FOUR

Full Fathom Five

Jokey was not usually a biting dog, but she was terrified. Pressed flat and combed out by the wind, she hung to the bare crag by the skin of her teeth while the thunder — which she dreaded more than anything in the world — absolutely cascaded round her trembling body. Her wildered eyes were rolling with fright and her long tongue lapped the terror. She clung for life to the summit of Rockall, behind the Master.

When he stepped back, he trod on her.

She bit him in the ankle.

Off balance, caught by a gust, tripped by the dog, the frail bundle of ancient bones spun through half a turn and landed on its hip.

This made a sharp crack, as loud as breaking a piece of firewood.

Jokey, shattered by what she had done as well as by the tempest, scrambled for the hangar.

Nicky stood passively, waiting to be told what to do.

After a few moments, in a pause between the thunder claps, the Master began to laugh.

247

It was a surprising laugh — strong and full-bodied and amused. It was a young man's laughter from the House of Fame, recorded there in 1820.

As it rang joyfully round the cliff-top, Nicky began to come alive. The catherine-wheel of the searchlight retracted, twinned, became blue eyes, was ordinary. He was looking at an old man with a broken pelvis, stretched at his feet.

The Master said, teasing him, with no difficulty about speaking:

> *"Now my charms are all o'erthrown,*
> *And what strength I have's mine own,*
> *Which is most faint."*

Seeing that the quotation was above the boy's head, he amused himself by adding a further one.

> *"'Ban, 'Ban, Cacaliban*
> *Has a new master — Get a new man . . .*
> *Farewell, master; farewell, farewell!"*

Nicky said, "Are you hurt? Can I help?"

"No."

"I could fetch Mr. Frinton to carry you down in the lift."

"*Let be.*"

"Shall I bring some whisky?"

"*The whole butt, man: my cellar is in a rock by the sea-side, where my wine is hid.*"

I suppose that is a quotation too, he thought vaguely, going down to get it in a daze. He noticed that the wind pressure had lessened, though the storm was still high. As he went, the Master called after him.

"*Marvellous sweet music.*"

There was a disc on the radiogram already. He started it at full volume before he brought the liquor back. On second thoughts, he threw the casement open. The peacock feathers and pampas grass rustled in the clean wind that came in. The disc was the fourth movement of Tchaikovsky's Fifth Symphony.

The Master had made himself comfortable. He knocked off the neck of the bottle, poured it down his throat and settled to listen.

The tremendous music was tattered by the dying gale. It came up in gusts from the shaking rock beneath them. The white-caps of the saga-haunted sea, trailing their gauzy drapery, went past processionally to its heave and thunder. The zaz and rumble of the elements began to fade.

While they listened, the Master said two things — to himself. First he said, "*Thought is free.*" Later on, "*He that dies pays all debts.*" He folded his hands on the alpenstock.

The theme of the first movement blazed out in the major key, while the old man smiled and nodded. There was nothing left to say.

No, there was one thing, and he said it.

He hauled himself up the alpenstock.

"*You do look, my son, in a moved sort,*
  As if you were dismay'd: be cheerful, sir.
  Our revels now are ended. These our actors,

The Master

As I foretold you, were all spirits, and
Are melted into air, into thin air:
And like the baseless fabric of this vision,
The cloud-capp'd towers, the gorgeous palaces,
The solemn temples, the great globe itself,
Yea, all which it inherits, shall dissolve,
And, like this insubstantial pageant faded,
Leave not a rack behind."

It was his will which took the halting body to the precipice.

The Master struck clear water in a sheet of spray which rose to meet him. It was a sheer drop.

And that was that — Full Fathom Five.

CHAPTER THIRTY-FIVE

Home Sweet Home

THE stable at Gaunt's Godstone was one of those whistling places where — to the clink of a hoof or the clank of a bucket — you suddenly hear a stable boy unexpectedly whistling *Non piu andrai* or *La ci darem*, and doing it accurately.

It was a bright, autumn morning, the leaves thinking of going golden on the trees and the clear sun thinking of taking to himself a touch of frost at sunrise. The hedges were the colour of woodsmoke.

The Duke came in to a late breakfast from cub-hunting, stamping his boots on the kitchen mat and whistling his favourite piece from *Iolanthe*. Later in the day he would have to rally the family, so that they could sell booklets to trippers and take them round the bedrooms of the mansion. (Yes, madam, that is our mother's coronet, but please use the ashtrays provided, if the customers have left any.) For the time being, since the house did not open till the buses arrived at eleven-thirty, his home was still his own — although he did have to live in the stables of it. He was whistling,

Nothing venture, nothing win.
Blood is thick but water's thin

In for a penny, in for a pound.
It's love that makes the world go round.

"So it does," said Mr. Frinton, looking fierce and comical in his skull cap and piratical whiskers.

"What, my dear fellar, still eating?"

They all were.

"Pinkie has gone to the house," said Judy, "to get the catalogues ready. He wants to be allowed to dress up in the footman's uniform, like the picture by Hogarth."

"If he wants to."

"He likes dressing up and it might sell some catalogues. Could Nicky and I be pages, do you think?"

"We could carry the Lothian Duchess's stuffed parrot."

"I won't have the parrot knocked about. It is coming to bits already."

"Then may I put on the Cromwell armour?"

"No."

"It seems to me," said Nicky gloomily, "that we were better off on the island. Everything here is 'Don't Touch'."

"Nicky."

"Oh, all right. I'm sorry."

"On the island," said Mr. Frinton, to keep the peace, "you had nothing to dress up in, except night-shirts."

"Thanks to Judy."

"Thanks to you."

"How can it be thanks to me when it is females who

are supposed to do the mending? Can it, Daddy?"

"I don't know what you are talking about."

"Judy said . . ."

"I didn't."

He began to swell like a persecuted toad.

"You . . ."

"Do you know," said Mr. Frinton, putting the marmalade between them to prevent a fight, "while all those bods on the island were nattering about Napoleon, I had a quotation from him up my sleeve, but I was too shy to use it."

"What?"

"He once said: 'One never does the same thing twice in a century.'"

"And what did he mean by that?" inquired the Duke, interested, holding a forkful of kedgeree two inches from his moustache.

"I think he meant that Hitler has used up dictatorships till about the year 2045. The Master would never have pulled it off."

"Interesting, very."

"But you didn't know the Master," said Nicky.

"I am thankful to say, not."

"If you had known him, you wouldn't be so sure."

"Sure of what?"

"Sure he couldn't have pulled it off, like Mr. Frinton said."

"Like Napoleon said," said Judy primly.

"Like Mr. Frinton says Napoleon said, you ape."

"Nicholas, you are not to call your sister an ape."

"Oh, hell," began Nicky. "Everybody . . ."

"Don't swear, and get on with your breakfast."

"One of the bad things," remarked Judy, "about the adventure was that it was sort of pointless. I mean, he ought to have been conquered by a hero or something. A knight in shining armour. It seems so . . . kind of untidy. Untidy that he should just trip over a dog."

"It was very tidy indeed," said Mr. Frinton.

"How?"

"When you are over-human, you can be caught by the under-human. He forgot that. And Time and Chance happen to all men."

"He had the humans fixed anyway."

"All of them."

"Another thing," said Mr. Frinton. "Do you realize that Totty was very clever after all?"

"How?"

"He saw it from the first. That was why he kidnapped Jokey. To use."

A devilish scheme had come to the sulking Nicky, to do with a joke which he had once seen in the papers.

"I suppose," he said craftily, "your shining hero would have spent all the time calling you Fair Lady?"

"Yes, he would. Why not? Everybody isn't rude like . . ."

"Then you'd better marry a bus-conductor."

"Why?"

"Fare, lady! Fares please! Fare, lady! Tuppenny bus! Tuppenny bus!"

And he began beating the top of a boiled egg with his teaspoon

"Beast!"

"Mike wye fer the Duchess of Straphanger!"

"I'll kill you . . ."

Mr. Frinton said, "Here's the post."

It was the post — and Mrs. Henderson delivered it with the milk as projected — and in it there was a letter in a strange handwriting, postmarked from Lerwick, addressed to Major-General the Duke of Lancaster, M.F.H.

"There," said Judy, when it had been opened.

Now Gilbert and Sullivan, who understood the rules of tragedy as perfectly as Aristotle did, once invented a nautical villain whose sole and frightful villainy was to say "I told you so." Judy could do this, just at Nicky's moment of triumph.

It was the famous letter in the bottle, looking as crisp as the day it was posted.

"Even if . . ."

"Well?"

"Even if it did get here," he said desperately, "it wasn't any good, because it was too late, and because . . ."

"Because what?"

"Because we had done everything before it came and even if it did come nobody could have done anything from this end and . . ."

"You *said* it wouldn't come."

"I didn't."

"You did."

"I said . . ."

"Too squeaky, I expect."

"Too what?"

"That Latin thing."

"Oh!" squealed Nicky, goaded beyond endurance. He blew himself up like the frog in Aesop, searching for the curse to end all curses. Everybody was against him. Everything was unfair. He was left to conquer Masters single-handed, the only survivor of the gallant band. He was expected to fight against hypnotism and thought transference and people of a hundred and fifty-seven and goodness knows what else. When he did work the Bus Conductor joke, the bottle had to arrive. Thwarted at every turn, unappreciated, actually locked up by his own friends, given no gratitude, treated as if he was *twelve* — yes, twelve, for they had reached thirteen the day before — what was the point of life? What availed the sceptred race? Where was justice? Why did anybody ever invent women? Where were the eagles and the trumpets? Who . . .

Eagles?

Napoleon.

He had got it.

He turned upon his quailing twin and gave her with majesty the full one-two.

"You are," said he, "a *Napoleonic nowt*."

Under the breakfast table, where she was messily munching, Jokey growled in sympathy when they raised their voices.

It was a Wednesday. Her troubles were over.

She was probably the only dog in history who has altered the destiny of the human race, so it is nice to know that they had given her a whole kipper.